FLUFFY BUNNY

BOOK 2: THE RUNESPELL SERIES

SARAH BUHRMAN

ISBN: 978-1-61296-973-2
PUBLISHED BY BLACK ROSE WRITING
www.blackrosewriting.com

Printed in the United States of America
Suggested retail price $17.95

Fluffy Bunny is printed in Adobe Caslon Pro

To my hubby (again): Stormie you are my alpha reader and my best friend. I couldn't do this without you.

To my editor, Courtney Cannon: You make me work too hard... lol

To my many beta readers: All of you are the bestestest! Thank you!

To my VPA, Tamara, I wouldn't have nearly this much time to write if you weren't doing what you do so well.

FLUFFY BUNNY

CHAPT 1

I stepped into my bedroom, my thick black hair still dripping from my shower, and froze at the sight of the three women waiting for me. The shock of finding someone in my room drained the heat of the shower from my body. Then I saw – really saw – the women, registered their appearance, and I felt a deep horror wash over me, numbing my limbs the way I imagined a mouse felt seconds before being swallowed whole by a snake.

The women were neither young nor old; not pretty, not ugly. They were average-looking women until I met their eyes. They looked at me in a slightly off-focus way, like a blind person, meeting my gaze without really seeing with those gray-ringed pupils that I found myself staring into.

I felt a slight burning on my chest, and I reached up to touch one of the four silver sigils hanging from my neck by a length of the chain that bound Fenrir Odinslayer, the monstrous wolf-son of Loki. The sigils were Runespells, my souvenirs from several months ago when I won a race for the powerful amulets.

After searching for my missing step-sister, I ended up fighting demons for the Runespells to keep a horrid man, not-so-good ol' Bob, from using them to cause trouble in the form of starting Ragnarok, the Norse end of the world. I wasn't sure how Bob would have done that, but I knew that Ragnarok was supposed to begin when Loki gets angry and breaks free from his chains to lead an army of Jotun, fire and ice giants, against Asgard.

None of that would end well.

I stopped not-so-good ol' Bob, fought off the demons, found the Runespells, and spent half a week in the hospital afterwards. My reward was to keep the Runespells, so I could use them in my search for the other fourteen missing sigils. Some prizes aren't worth the trouble.

As my fingertips grazed the sigil tingling against my skin, information flooded into my mind, telling me about the god-creatures before me, and I understood why I'd felt such primal fear at their gaze.

The women before me were not gods, after all. They were stronger than the gods. They were god-creatures that I would never want to anger or insult. They were beings that I would normally think long and hard about dealing with before I would even consider bringing myself to their attention. Only I didn't get a warning for this encounter. I didn't get any time to prepare myself, mentally or emotionally, for them.

They were the Norns, and they had come to see me.

•   •   •

They spoke, all three at once, with the same words, but each had a different rhythm and sound to her voice. The effect was uncomfortable in a way that made my ears hurt and my mind flinch away.

The one standing closest to the door, to my right, had a voice like a snake shedding its skin in dry leaves and dead grass. Her voice was slow and even. Unstoppable. It sounded parched and brittle, reminding me of the death before rebirth. If I had to pick one as the oldest of the three, it would be her with a dull, scaly look to her skin.

The middle one stood straight upright, her face ageless and severe. Her voice was firm, a clipped monotone, the way I imagined a single-minded cybernetic creature would sound while explaining with cold logic that the human race was to host the next generation of their kind, and that fighting this fate would be a waste of energy.

The last of the three lounged against my dresser with bright, languid eyes and a small, unpleasant smile on her large, moist red lips. The sound that passed those lips was that of sweaty sex mixed with the bloody squish of a blade thrust into a human abdomen.

"The Weaving is threatened. Souls are not passed on as they should be. The half-corpse will cut short threads needed to form the Pattern. You will restore the balance."

I clutched the towel wrapped around my torso, holding it close around my body, defensively, like the energy I had drawn up in a reflexive shield. My gaze shot to the bathrobe laying on the top of the dresser, just inches from the third Norn's elbow. I considered walking over and putting it on, but my whole body lurched at the idea of moving closer to them. I kept my feet from fleeing by a tiny margin. I turned back to the Norns, opened my mouth and croaked out a wordless sound.

This pissed me off. Damned gods. They showed up and did their best to scare the crap out of you – and, to be fair, they did a good job of that. Then they just had to speak in riddles, as if making something even harder to understand was part of their job description.

The flare of annoyance helped me swallow the dryness in my throat so I could speak, and I fell back on my usual defense. Sarcasm. "Can you say that again, this time without the code-talk for us mortals who haven't taken Cryptic Godspeak 101?"

As soon as the words left my lips, I realized what I'd done. Panic drained the little remaining warmth from my body. I clamped my jaw shut, snapping my teeth together on the tip of my tongue. I tasted blood and my shoulders sagged in defeat, certain my lippy-ness had finally gotten me killed.

The three women stared at me for a moment. When they finally spoke, I was so tense, I actually jumped at the sound. "It was not an exaggeration, what we've heard of your sharp and brazen tongue."

They shifted, each moving only a little, but I flinched back as if they had outright attacked.

They continued speaking in their weird, not quite in sync way. "There is a group of people who live near the place called Santa Fe. They are a healing commune known as The Rod of Asclepius. This group cures people of illnesses that would otherwise cut their threads..."

The women glanced at each other as if discussing their next move, then turned their dead, gray eyes back to me. "The souls are destined to go to Hel's domain, as is her due. She is angry that so many are denied to her. She has declared that we must put this right or she will collect the souls herself."

I blinked, filtering through the words. "So, the goddess of the dead is pissed that a bunch of people aren't dying? And she's, what... going to start killing random people?"

The three nodded in unison. "She cannot do this. The Pattern cannot bear such chaos at this time. The Weaving will unravel."

"The Weaving?" I frowned. Many religions had some sort of story about the tapestry of the world or of fate, or whatever. The threads were the people and events. It was a metaphor for... "Are you saying reality could fall apart?"

"That is a simple, but adequate understanding."

I suddenly felt dizzy. I stumbled over to my bed and dropped onto it as my legs gave out. Ragnarok was one thing, but if reality started to fall apart, that was even worse.

Reality was how we saw the world. And how the world saw us. From a magical perspective, it was more of an agreement on how things should work than an immutable law. It kept things more or less sane.

A breakdown in reality could result in literally anything. Unicorns appearing. Demons roaming the Earth - well, more openly than usual. Even the most horrible and fantastical imaginings of artists and authors could simply start to exist.

I certainly wasn't prepared to deal with Cthulhu and his buddies. Or for the world in the paintings of Salvador Dali to replace the laws of Physics.

I looked up to find the three terrible women standing over me. Their faces were – not softer, certainly not empathetic, but perhaps less terror-inducing.

I swallowed. "Is this about the Runespells? Are you saying someone is using one of them?"

The three seemed to exchange glances without moving their eyes as they watched me. The effect made my stomach roil. "This we do not know," the robotic one said.

"It is possible," the brittle one hissed.

The one with the red lips licked a circle around her mouth. "Possible enough for us to be able to call on you for this quest."

I frowned. That sounded a bit too much like a loophole to me.

"You must stop this from happening. You are the hero. You are called upon." The trio of women said in their not quite synchronized way. I nodded my understanding. This was what I'd agreed to last time. My vacation was over.

I closed my eyes against the emotions that swept over me. I was pretty resentful, mostly, though there was a healthy dose of hate and fear, and even a small touch of pride at being the hero – cue the trumpets. But resentment was the big one. I resented the gods, mostly, for their actions which placed the Runespells where they could be misused by humans wanting to trigger Ragnarok. Especially Odin.

The Allfather wasn't the only player involved, but he had the advantages of his information-gathering ravens, Huginn and Muninn, and the knowledge of the future gained from his sacrifice of an eye to the Well of Mimir at the roots of Yggdrasil. The same well where my current guests spent their days. Of all the gods and god-creatures, Odin was the one who should have seen this whole thing coming.

I opened my eyes and found myself alone.

Perfect. I guess I had to figure out the rest of my quest on my own.

I heaved a sigh. *Gods.*

CHAPT 2

It didn't take me long to find the commune the Norns had been talking about. The Rod of Asclepius Healing Center had a website that was going viral on social media. Apparently, they were almost as popular as "super-foods as a panacea" recommended by social media commenters and positive-thinking gurus. The Prophet Zaro and his wife, Nancy Gaona, the couple who ran the Center, were becoming a real New Age phenomenon.

I gathered as much information as I could before I called up my only police contact, Detective Brett Ames. I needed to know about going undercover, and I was pretty sure an internet search wasn't going to have the little tips that could save my butt.

"Shit," Ames answered the phone.

"Well, hey to you, too," I shot back. I didn't blame him. I didn't exactly bring sunshine and rainbows into his life.

"What do you want?" he growled.

"I just need some tips on going undercover," I said, keeping my tone light. "You know, faking belief in ideals, living contrary to my moral code. That kind of thing."

The line was silent for a long moment.

"Dammit, Nicola," he said, huffing out a breath. "You don't have the training for that kind of thing. It takes months, years to do that stuff."

"Yeah," I said. "But the ones that have undercover training can't handle the crap you know I'm gonna find there."

Ames sighed. "Don't I know it." He fell quiet for a moment. "First off, you usually need someone to get you in. An inside man, so to speak. They give you a certain cred within the organization, and they eliminate a lot of the questions and some of the initial testing."

"That could be a problem," I said. "I don't know anyone there."

"Where you going? What's the target?" Ames shot the questions out with a bite that showed how upset he was.

"The Rod of Asclepius Healing Center, Sante Fe, New Mexico."

"You're kidding."

"No," I paused. "You heard of it?"

The phone crackled and snuffled as Ames shifted it around. "I got a cousin, Sandy, out that way. Her daughter joined that Center a few months ago. She's been worried 'cause Lupé hasn't been calling or anything." He paused. "I told her it was probably okay."

I could hear Ames cussing under his breath. "Lupé won't trust me since she knows I'm a cop, so I can't help you there."

I nodded, then realized he couldn't see me. "I understand," I said aloud. Then I hesitated. "Do you want me to find Lupé? Check up on her and stuff?"

Ames' voice was low, almost inaudible, and gruff. "Yeah, thanks."

"Okay," I said. "I'll do everything I can for her." I put all the assurance I could into my voice.

•   •   •

Ames gave me a few more pointers, but mostly it came down to: don't lie if you don't have to. Lies are easy to forget. Keeping things close to the truth keeps you from messing up the story.

After going through the website with a critical eye, I signed up for a weekend seminar at the Center, hoping that would be enough to get my foot in the door, and bought a one-way ticket to Santa Fe. The Center had a shuttle to pick up visitors from the airport, and I made sure that I was on the list for that. I hoped that the lack of an easy exit would help keep me in the place.

I left Ella with my mother. Again. After what happened six months ago, they both watched me with sad eyes, but they didn't ask questions. I gave my mother everything she would need in case... but I assured them I would be back as soon as I could.

I held onto Ella extra long, this time knowing some of the dangers that might await me. Her small arms clung to me, and I let her hang on until she was ready to let go. As her arms slipped away from my neck, an empty feeling grew in my gut.

I set my jaw, and the tears didn't fall until I was halfway to the airport.

● ● ●

I walked through the airport, still feeling the effects of leaving my little girl once again, and looking for someone holding up one of those ridiculous signs you see in the movies. The website actually had a picture of a pretty blonde in a cream linen blouse holding the sign so we could see what to look for. I had never really considered that people actually used those things, but, given the late-afternoon crowd, I could see how they helped people find their connection if they'd never met.

A man in a business suit shoved past me, nearly knocking me over, dragging his wheeled suitcase behind him. And, just like that, I felt it return. Like warm oatmeal climbing up my spine and filling my ears before warming my cheeks and coloring the edges of my vision with a pinkish red.

During that hellish week six months ago, I'd lost it. I'd snapped from the stress and tried to beat the crap out of one of the walls of our then-prison. My vision had gone red, my ears had filled with a roaring sound, and I had literally lost control of myself, hitting the drywall until my hands were so battered they went numb. It had been a terrifying experience.

The worst part was that Mercy and Joseph had been right there. They saw, or rather heard in the darkness, what had happened, and they had cared for me after I'd passed out. I'd never lost control so badly before in my life, and it was... shameful.

Mercy had acted odd about it, but not in the way I would have expected. She seemed to be implying there was something important about my loss of control. She hadn't brought it up since, though, and I wasn't eager to replay the experience, so I was still in the dark about whatever she had been thinking.

Unfortunately, the past was not staying in the past.

Since that time, I'd been having these random bouts of – well, losing my temper. Not like people pushing and pushing until I snapped at them. More like people doing normal, crappy people things

– cutting me off in traffic, bumping into me on a busy sidewalk, not holding the door when I was walking right behind them – just normal, inconsiderate stuff. And I'd lose it. Not every time. Not even most of the time. Not when I was especially stressed or anything like that. Just completely, spin of the wheel, roll of the dice, random times.

It scared the crap out of me.

I stood still, taking deep breaths, my hands shaking, as I pushed the warm feeling down and away.

Crap, crap, crap, crap, crap... Deep breaths. De-e-e-e-e-ep breaths. Don't let me lose it. Please, don't let me lose it.

The warmth in my ears finally left, and I could feel the warm-oatmeal rage-lava draining down the back of my throat. My spine still tingled from the after-effects of the feeling, but I was no longer fighting the rage.

I sighed and shook my head, blinking away the stress tears from my eyes. Now that it was gone, I could admit that I had been inches away from chasing that man down and doing my very best to beat him to a pulp with his suitcase. Such an irrational and stupid reaction. Yeah, the guy was being a jerk, but he didn't deserve what I would have done.

I stood still a moment longer, making sure I had myself under control. I looked up to see a Hispanic woman in her early twenties wearing a white maxi-dress and staring at me with wide eyes. There were three men and two women standing with her, holding bags and shifting their weight from one foot to the other. A brief glimpse at their energies showed that the bystanders were an anxious orange. The woman, however, was simply wary. Calm, but alert.

I blinked as I realized that the large object she was holding was a sign that read "Asclepius Center Shuttle." I approached the group, grimacing to myself at the first impression I'd given them.

"Are you going to the Center?" The woman watched me carefully, despite the warm smile she gave me.

I nodded. "I'm taking a workshop," I croaked, my throat still tight from my incident.

She pulled a pocket-sized notebook and a highlighter pen out of the large bag slung across her chest. "What's your name?"

"Nicola," I said. "Last name, Crandall."

She scanned the page, juggling the sign, notebook, and pen with a practiced grace. She took the lid of the pen in her teeth and pulled it off to highlight a line before putting it back on and dropping both the notebook and pen back into her bag.

She met my eyes with less hesitation than before, and with more compassion. "Welcome, then. It seems you may need us more than you may realize. My name is Lupé."

• • •

I unpacked my small suitcase, stuffing the clothes into the tiny dresser in the miniscule room. It was practically a dorm room, complete with a super-single bed with a mattress on one of those platform bed frames with uncomfortable looking springs going across it. The type you find in dorms, camping cabins, and prisons.

I wasn't even assuming that that's what the bed was because I could see it; the bed had come with the room, some assembly required. The first thing I'd done when I was shown my room was to take the mattress that had been leaning against the wall and put it down on the frame. The thin, worn bed sheets went on next, though I took extra time to frown at the lumpy, flat pillow. I was used to three pillows tucked around me at night, a carry-over from an uncomfortable pregnancy

I sighed. The two drawer dresser was barely two foot wide. My clothes, packed to save space, barely fit. I wedged the last pair of panties into the top drawer. Apparently, changes of clothing weren't a priority for this group.

I sat on the bed to consider my position. I spoiled myself at home, making sure that Ella and I were always comfortable in our retreat from the world. This little venture was going to be rough.

It wasn't going well, so far. I knew that much. After my near rage episode at the airport, I hadn't had any chance to talk to Lupé without the other workshop attendees listening in. I had promised Ames I'd make sure she was okay. To do that with no authority or causing suspicion meant making friends. I needed to step up my game.

Or change it.

I considered the thought. I'd intended to prove myself worthy of being welcomed into the Center's core group. But that was a slim possibility, since I didn't know what the group leaders would be looking for. If I went with a different tactic, I might have a better chance.

Groups like this were always looking for recruits. But, if, as I suspected, they were more cultish than the healing circles I was used to, they might be looking less for confidence and more for the lost soul type. Given the emotional fallout of my previous experiences, playing the poor unfortunate would be easy. I'd just have to let my fears and insecurities show more.

The hard part would be doing that without letting them overwhelm me. I fell back on the mattress, wincing at a bent spring poking me in the ribs. I couldn't say I felt better about this idea, but I certainly felt more like I wasn't going to immediately fail.

CHAPT 3

I stared down at my food with a feeling of panic rising inside. It was my first meal at the Rod of Asclepius Healing Center, and it wasn't looking like the food I was used to. There was a sweet potato mash with a drizzle of olive oil, brown rice with shredded carrots, and a selection of raw fresh fruits. It looked and smelled really good, too.

I leaned over to my neighbor, a middle-aged woman with the slightly leathery, tanned face of an outdoor lover for life. "Is this... vegan?" I asked, trying to keep the horror from my voice.

"Of course," she murmured. "Animal-based foods conflict with the healing energies, so we don't use them."

"Oh," I replied. I picked up the fork and dug in.

"Eating animals lowers your energies," she continued. "It weighs you down."

I nodded. That was what I liked about meat and starchy foods. It grounded me in a way that felt comfortable and, in many ways, necessary.

"We prefer foods that are based on a light energy that doesn't encumber our souls."

I nodded again, letting the woman talk. It was something I'd heard many times in many ways before.

I'd always been a meat eater. I'd tried to go vegetarian once, but what started out as vegetarian quickly became lacto-ovo-vegetarian as I added back eggs and my beloved cheeses. Only a few months passed before chicken crept back in, too. The first time my mother served prime rib, a holiday treat, beef was back, and bacon was too tempting to last more than half a year.

Don't get me wrong. The fact that I love these foods had a lot to do with it, but I had also been irritable, distracted, and prone to bouts of low moods the entire time. It isn't just that I crave meat. I don't function well without it.

From a spiritual standpoint, I understood the argument. Meat and starches weighed the energies down. For some people, that was too heavy. For me, it was like the weights on a hot air balloon, holding it in place and even giving it direction when it was flying. Without the weight, my mind was quickly lost in space. Apparently, there's some scientific reason for all of that, too, but I couldn't recall the physiological descriptions and biochemical names.

I recognized that my thoughts were focused on food. It was no wonder, considering I hadn't eaten much today except for the free nuts on the plane. I'd been too upset about leaving Ella to eat breakfast, and options for lunch had been over-priced, poor quality burgers at the airport, so I skipped that.

I ate the entire meal, which was quite delicious, and scraped the plate clean. I was still hungry. I realized this was going to be a long stay. As I scratched at a tiny smear of sweet potato with my fork, I wondered if it would be in bad form to ask for the second course.

The room suddenly went from muted to dead silent.

A man stood on the stage at the end of the room. He was good-looking in that well-groomed and not hideous kind of way, like a catalog model. Nothing particularly special, but nice to look at.

His dark hair was styled in a modern parted fashion, and his outfit was a long white linen tunic with a Mandarin collar and matching loose pants. The white of his clothing contrasted nicely with the deep tan of his skin.

The man spread his arms out as if to embrace the entire room. His head dropped back and he stared at the ceiling. He stood that way for several minutes. His audience stared, afraid to look away and miss what came next.

"Enlightenment!" he cried.

Several people jumped at the sudden sound.

The man's head jerked upright and he stared around the room. One arm stretched out in front of him, moving in an arc with his gaze.

"That is what we seek, is it not?" he asked.

There were soft murmurs of agreement from the crowded room.

"We want love," the man, who I assumed was Zaro, continued.

"We want peace. We want compassion. We want..." he dragged the words out into a pause filled with tension and anticipation, "...understanding."

The man paced to one corner of the stage. "We want to know what we are here for, right? We want to know our purpose, don't we?"

I could feel myself being drawn in by his words. My experiences had taught me that gods are real, but it hadn't clued me in on any of life's deeper secrets. I had no idea if I was on the right path. And I did want to know. I did want peace and understanding.

The man walked with a measured stride across the front of the stage. "That is why we are all here, isn't it? That's why we've come here?"

Several people called out "Yes!"

He paused and flashed a boyish grin. "Well, some of you come for the delicious sweet potato pudding, am I right?"

I laughed softly with the crowd, knowing the man was charming us. Part of my mind warned me. This was typical self-help speak. When done well, it would excite the audience. It would capture them. But my thoughts were muddled by my own doubts, and distracted by the humor and the slight hunger ache in my stomach.

The man walked back to the center of the stage.

"Our guests this weekend will be getting their first taste of the peace and knowledge that we can give them," he said. His voice was calm but he projected well. "But first, our evening tradition, and a little hint of what they can look forward to."

A girl of maybe fourteen years appeared at the edge of the stage. She looked terrified to be in front of so many people, but she approached the man without hesitation. He gestured to her, opening one arm to her, and she fell to her knees at his feet. The man smiled with pleasure and compassion.

A jolt ran through me at the wrongness of what I was seeing. That type of behavior, the girl's and Zaro's both, was a pretty big red flag for cultish situations. Having dealt with the nearly constant question of whether Pagan groups were cults, I'd become fairly well educated on the true signs of cultism. However, my current situation being what it was, I tried not to focus on that line of thought.

The man held up his hands in supplication. Then he reached for the girl with one hand while the other clutched at something hanging from his neck. The girl stared up at him, trembling visibly. His hand brushed her cheek, and her head fell back.

I could see her eyes were closed, and a soft smile lifted her lips. The trembling stopped, and her contented sigh echoed in the silent room. I let my eyes go loose, to change my vision, to see the energies at play. It took me a moment to work out what I was seeing.

The girl was swathed in the most gorgeous white-blue, like huge, fluffy clouds on a warm sunny day, shot through with dark colored streaks so thin, I couldn't tell what the color was. I'd never seen someone so completely...

Happy was the wrong word. It was too active. This wasn't active. This was soft and passive. Purely receptive and accepting. It was reading by a fireplace. It was sprawled across a comfy bed. It was being surrounded by the people you want to be surrounded by. It was hot chocolate and fresh bread, sweet tea and strawberries.

Scandinavian countries had a word for it: hygge. In the English language, we settle for words like comfortable or content.

And it was billowing out of the man's hand. His touch was giving her this feeling, feeding it to her soul.

My stomach wrenched, hunger combined with nausea. But it was a brief reaction, suppressed by an overwhelming desire. I knew what I wanted, since the pressures and responsibilities of parenthood had settled over my shoulders like weights. I knew what I needed and craved from the time I'd accepted the mantle and burden of being "hero" to the gods' quest. I knew what I had been looking for, in one way or another, for my entire adult life.

I wanted that touch.

• • •

When I got back to my tiny room, I pulled a digital recorder out of my underwear drawer. I couldn't call up Joseph and talk things out with him, which was my first choice. But I could talk to myself and record it to go over again later.

I lay back on the uncomfortable bed and thought about what had happened for a moment. Then I hit the record button.

"I don't know how to explain this... thing that has happened, so I'll just start from the beginning. I'm here because I'm searching for something. I'm not sure where it is or who can help me, but I know it's here."

I shifted on the bed, the discomfort more from my thoughts than from random bed springs poking into my back. I noticed a slight, musty smell wafting around me, and I grimaced.

"I keep thinking about what happened six months ago. It's like a record playing in my head. If I see or hear something, it might start the record playing. If I'm in a certain mood, it might trigger the record to play.

"It's always the same thing that I focus on, though. Did I do alright?"

I heaved a sigh, getting lost in the memories.

"Obviously, to a point, I did. I'm still alive. So is Joseph, Ames, Hound Dog. Even those people at the grain elevator made it out on their own two feet. Even if we were all a little beat up.

"That's got to be some kind of miracle. I didn't think we all would make it out alive. I was so scared because I didn't want anyone to die."

I grimaced, remembering the battle and the flames. The smell of sweat and flour. The clanging of weapons and equipment rattling. I could almost taste the bitter saltiness from the ash that had filled the air. And I could see the sympathy on Mercy's face when she told me about the body they didn't find.

"Except for him. I wanted him to die. I feel like crap just saying that, but it's true. I wanted him to die, and I don't think he did."

I rolled over, wincing at whatever was digging into my hip. I shifted around until the pain disappeared.

"Now I've got this other issue. This Center does this healing stuff, and with pretty miraculous results, if I understand correctly. But some... well, some people - kind of - they don't like what's going on."

I frowned. My head felt fuzzy, and it was hard to stay focused. My stomach growled, roiling in my gut.

"I need to get to the bottom of this. For me. I need to prove to myself that the thing before wasn't just dumb luck, that I can do this whole hero gig.

"I need to understand what is happening. I need to be able to use my mind to figure things out. That's where I work the best. That's my comfort zone."

I bit my lip, thinking about how the day had ended. I could feel my thoughts being drawn to the memory of the girl and the energy around her.

"As for that display at supper, I just... I don't know what to make of it. That guy - I'm assuming he's Zaro Gaona, part of the couple that runs the Center - he would have made Tony Robbins proud. He had everyone excited, anticipating his next move, his next words. He had us primed."

I sighed and let my head fall against my arm.

"Crap. Us. Yeah, I was excited, too. Despite knowing what he was doing, I was just as eager as the rest of them."

I rolled back to my back, waving my hands around for emphasis. Yeah, I really got into talking to myself.

"Then that girl came out. It was weird, disturbing, the way she threw herself at his feet. I can't imagine ever doing that, no matter how awesome the person seems to be. Hells, I didn't even do that when I was faced with actual gods."

I smiled at the memory of Odin's face when I had stood up to him pressuring me. The smile turned into a grimace. He could have had a different reaction. He could have punished or even killed me for being so bold in the face of a deity.

But he didn't. And I'm not sure I'd have done anything different, even in retrospect. It was just part of my nature.

I turned my thoughts back to the energy display.

"That energy Zaro gave her was... just, wow. It was so beautiful. White-blue, soft and warm. I know she was feeling a level of comfort, of contentment, that I have only wished for my entire life."

I shook my head in disbelief of what I'd seen.

"And I know I'm not alone. Most people will never feel that in their lives. Total peace and relaxation aren't common enough for most people to ever experience it. But that's what I saw.

"Now that I think about it, though, there were streaks in the energy, too. I should know what those are."

My stomach growled again, shooting sharp, crampy pains through my gut.

"Dammit, these stomach cramps are so distracting." I sighed. "Maybe I should just try to get some sleep."

I got up to put the recorder back in the drawer. A knock at my door startled me. I dropped the recorder among the socks and panties and tossed a few pieces of cloth over top of it before closing the drawer.

I cracked open the door and peeked out. "Yes?"

Lupé stood in the hallway, looking both serene and anxious at the same time. "I was wondering if you would like to talk."

I quickly opened the door all the way and gestured for her to come in. "Make yourself comfortable," I said, then frowned at the only place to sit – the bed.

Lupé caught my look and grinned. "It takes some getting used to, doesn't it?"

I nodded and we sat down.

Lupé leaned forward, jumping right in. "Did you enjoy the display we had earlier? Some people don't really seem to understand what is happening, but I saw it on your face. You get it, don't you?"

I cleared my throat. "Well... I could see... Um..."

Lupé grasped my hand and patted it as if to reassure me. The oddity that a woman more than a decade younger than myself would act the part of the experienced older woman sat heavily in the back of my throat.

I set my jaw and, as Joseph would say, womaned up. "I could see the feeling, the energy, that he sent into the girl. It was like nothing I'd ever seen before," I admitted.

Lupé tilted her head. "You could see it? What do you mean?"

I sighed. Might as well go all the way with this. "I can see energy and emotions. It's like a color, but also like an after image, like when you look at a bright light and then look away?"

Lupé nodded.

"Well, that's how it looks, but there's more to it. I can see a texture, but it's more than texture. I can tell that the energy tonight was soft and warm. I got these associations that rounded it out: strawberries and cream, warm blankets, children snuggling together, puppies sleeping in a pile. Things like that.

"And it's like I can just almost feel the emotions that are there. It's very light, not like empathy, where I might take on those emotions. More like memories of emotions."

Lupé stared at me, watching my face. "And what did you think of the emotions Zaro gave to Emilia?"

I stared at the wall, not really seeing it as I let my mind go back to that moment when I'd almost felt what the girl had felt. "It was peace, comfort, contentment. To a degree that I've never seen before." I shook my head, trying to clear it. "It was... amazing."

Lupé smiled. "I should let Zaro know about your gift. It's always wonderful to have the addition of such talent at the Center, even if only for a weekend."

I hesitated, afraid to take the opportunity that had been laid out before me. I was afraid to appear too eager. "Well..." I let the word trail off.

Lupé raised her eyebrows. "Unless you had something else in mind."

I shrugged. "After what I've already seen, I might..." I paused.

Lupé leaned forward. "Yes?"

I shrugged. "I might consider, you know. Staying longer?" I sighed. "I don't know. Maybe you guys don't let just anyone join you. It's just that it feels so much like a welcoming place. Like it might be what I'm looking for."

I turned away, afraid she would see the lie, but more afraid that there was no lie to see.

Lupé reached out and laid her hand on my shoulder. "I'm sure that Zaro and Nancy will easily recognize that your spirit belongs with us." She smiled. "I'll help you find your place here."

Warmth ran through my body, the feeling of welcome from this young woman was so strong. When her hand withdrew and she left the room, bubbling with happiness, the cold fingers of dread crawled up my spine in its place.

CHAPT 4

The first morning, after a breakfast of delicious but animal-free oatmeal with real maple syrup and orange slices, the full dozen of us attending the weekend workshop were taken to a large room filled with benches that faced the short stage. It was like every single church I'd ever been in, only there was no altar on the stage and no crucifixion displayed.

I sat in the last row, right on the end, wrapping my arms around my complaining stomach. I wasn't looking forward to sitting through the workshop. I hadn't even noticed the topic, really. I'd just signed up for the first available spot to get me in.

Zaro stood up in front of the group, gesturing in the big, showy way he'd done last night.

"There is a secret!" he cried out, pausing dramatically. "There is a secret to controlling your anger."

I immediately perked up. This could be interesting after all.

"Anger can consume you. It can eat away at you. It can burn your spirit." He walked around the stage, gesturing with wide arms. "How many times have you felt... trapped? Trapped by the anger in your heart and in your gut?"

Several of the people sitting around me murmured and nodded.

"How many times have you felt... controlled? Controlled by actions done in a moment, in a fit of rage?"

The murmurs were louder this time.

"This is your life! Your life! You need," he stretched out the E sound, "to take your life back! Take it back!"

A woman in the front row called out, "Yes!"

"Take back your life!"

More of the audience called out. "Yes!"

"It is yours! Take it back! Take back what is yours!"

Most of the audience was now calling out. "Take it back!" "My life!"

Zaro stopped in the center of the stage, head hanging down in front of him, arms stretched out in a stop signal. Everyone went silent. We all sat still, waiting for – anticipating – the next part of his message.

The silence stretched out. Someone coughed. A few people began moving restlessly in their seats. I suddenly realized that my butt had become the numb-sore that happens when you sit still for too long, so I shifted my weight around on the hard bench.

"Do get it? Do you really get it?" Zaro asked, his low voice drawing the audience's attention once more, drawling and so quiet I caught myself holding my breath to hear him. "Do you understand what you are committing to? Do you realize the step that you've taken in affirming that you will take your life back from anger?"

His head lifted and he stared intently into the small crowd. I noticed several people glancing away and shifting uncomfortably under his piercing gaze. His eyes fell on me, and I felt myself shrink from the intensity of his stare.

He dropped his hands and stepped forward. "Do you know what anger can do to you?"

He paused as if waiting for an answer, but no one spoke. "It lowers your energy," he said, measuring each word out. Pointing into the audience with one hand, then the other, and back, alternating with each statement.

"It takes the vitality from your body. It inhibits your immune system." He raised the volume of his voice as he continued. "It stops you from being able to use your energy... to do great things. It prevents you from reaching your full potential!"

I let my body fall back against the backrest of the bench. Now that he'd gotten into the real message of the workshop, I realized I'd heard this stuff before. It was all excitement in the beginning but ended with a long speech about how we were failing to live up to our potential greatness, and it wasn't our fault 'cause we got stuck.

It was the bread and butter of what my friends and I called "fluffy bunny" gurus. They were the ones who preached love and light until you wanted to throw up. They were usually white, middle class, and completely unaware of how often they dismissed the realities faced by minorities, disabled people, and other disenfranchised groups. In a word, they were privileged.

These fluffy bunnies were so named because one common belief was that nature was full of fluffy bunnies that were cuddly and cute and meant no one any harm, and pain and suffering were all the result of people and their meanness and their negative energies.

They never considered that people might be angry, depressed or bitter because shit happened that was out of everyone's control. They never thought that just thinking happy thoughts would never solve financial worries – these white light-bringers had never had serious financial woes, or suffered discrimination because of race, or struggled to learn in an inadequate school system with no funding because it was in the wrong part of town.

It wasn't really that there was anything wrong with the idea of positive thinking. It certainly had its place. It was just so very... biased. It only addressed half the story.

People were far more complicated than what a few mantras and some happy thoughts could address. And addressing social issues seemed to be completely out of reach for these techniques. They just weren't multi-dimensional enough to work in those situations.

Zaro was going over some techniques for how to "face down" and conquer your anger. It was the same stuff I'd been hearing for years from the same kind of self-help, New Agey types: breathe deeply, practice tolerance, express gratitude, exercise patience, find the humor. And, my all-time favorite, forgive.

I tried not to roll my eyes, thinking about the bouts of rage I'd been experiencing. I doubted that finding something to be grateful for would stop that. And the problem wasn't a matter of patience – it was too illogical for that to work.

Wanting to not completely waste the weekend, I decided I would at least try to meditate more often. I'd always been pretty sporadic about my meditations, and it couldn't hurt to focus on the calming practice.

"Tomorrow," Zaro said, catching my attention again. "We will be going over some specific exercises and techniques to control your anger and bring your life back under your control. Please, enjoy the rest of your day and feel free to explore the Center's many pleasurable features."

I waited until most of the audience had stood before I got up. A rush of blood left my head and dropped into my feet. I grabbed the backrest in front of me so I wouldn't stagger.

I shook my head a little. Apparently, the change in my diet and poor sleep last night on the lumpy mattress had affected me more than I'd realized. I tried to get the fuzzy feeling out of my head, but I still felt like a thin veil of cotton covered my mind.

A deep breath steadied my balance enough for me to move away from my seat and fall in line behind the rest of the group. My stomach growled loudly and I glanced around for a clock, but the walls were bare. I resigned myself to waiting longer for more food.

I followed the crowd to the huge gardens and paused outside the door, blinking in the bright light. The desert sunlight was more intense than I was used to without the tree-covered hills to diffuse it. There were some trees in the large space, but they were clustered in only a few spaces.

Most of the rich gardens were filled with gravel, Joshua trees, and cacti, or the typical, evenly spaced rows of vegetables. A few storage sheds broke up the stark beauty, and Center members in cream, tan and brown linen tunics and loose pants moved leisurely around the spaces, pulling weeds, carrying baskets of produce, and moving gravel around.

There were benches placed in particularly lovely areas, where Center members and workshop guests alike sat and enjoyed the scenery. I found an empty bench and sat down, looking absently at the energy of the dozens of people in the huge garden space.

Several of the "brothers" and "sisters" of the Center were surrounded by a blue-white cloud, much like the energy that Zaro had given the girl the previous night, only much less intense. Like her energy, their clouds were streaked with other feelings, but I still couldn't see the other emotion colors clearly enough to know what they were.

I let my eyes drift closed, and I tilted my head up to allow the sun to shine fully on my face. The heat seeped into my bones, chasing away the icy fears of my doubts. I took a deep breath and admitted to myself that this was a pleasant experience. There were worse ways to enjoy a weekend. There didn't seem to be anything to indicate malicious intent or abuse – or even use – of one of the Runespells. Yeah, Zaro was a pretty typical fluffy bunny guru, but that wasn't necessarily evil.

I opened my eyes and blinked away the after-image of the light burning through my eyelids. I felt my balance waver.

I must have been feeling a little lightheaded from the unusual diet and the heat of the sun. I stared at the tall trunks of the Joshua trees, covered with the fibrous bark that seemed to be something between spines and hair. The texture drew me in, and I lost track of time immersed in staring at the unusual plant.

"Hey."

I blinked and turned my head at the voice. I smiled up at the woman standing with the sun behind her.

"Mind if I sit?" she asked, with a familiar accent.

I nodded and gestured to the seat beside me.

The woman moved to sit beside me, and I realized the darkness of her face was not just because of the light shining at her back. Her skin was the deep, rich brown of dark umber. Her hair was ebony, and she had dozens of thick knots of black hair tightly braided and gathered close against her head, forming a kind of diamond pattern against her skull. The hairstyle was a great look for her, both fun and somehow strong.

I remembered that the style was called Bantu knots, and I briefly wondered what I would look like with my own thick, dark hair done like that.

I smiled at her again. "I'm Nicola."

She smiled back at me, though I noticed her expression was a little reserved. I blinked, checking out her energy. The woman glowed with a golden aura, showing a pleasing combination of confidence and compassion.

"My name is Kaitlyn," she said. "You must be with the weekend seminar, too."

I nodded. "Yeah. I'm not sure what to think about it, though."

"I hear ya," she said. "It's really interesting, but I'm not really sure about it... yet."

I noticed the accent again, and I tried to place it. "Where are you from? Your accent seems familiar."

She laughed. "I'm originally from New Orleans. If you ever watch any movies ever, you'd recognize the accent. Hollywood can't seem to get enough of it."

"Oh, yeah, I guess so," I said, grinning. "I've always wanted to visit New Orleans."

She laughed. "Everyone does."

"Kaitlyn, Nicola!" Lupé called. "There you two are. It's time for supper!"

I stood up and walked with Kaitlyn to the commons room, wondering how many vegetables would be sacrificed to me this meal.

● ● ●

That night, I slipped into the astral plane after I'd made a brief recording of my thoughts but before I could fall asleep. I wanted some real answers to why I was here, and I wasn't getting enough information in the physical realm.

I closed my eyes and focused on my breathing, concentrating on the in and out. I let the memories from my energy-seeing of the last few days flit through my mind: lacy-finned fish swimming in the clouds during my flight over the Midwest, a quetzalcoatl slithering its feathered body through the garden, a hummingbird made of transparent gemstones flitting through the airport parking lot.

The images and the breathing put me into a kind of trance, and I slipped into the astral plane. I barely noticed the desert-like surroundings or the dry air that sucked moisture from my throat.

Instead, I immediately jumped to the library setting where I focused on my searches for information. I tried calling for the knowledge, visualizing a book containing the facts that I sought, but no such text appeared in my hands.

I sighed. I could go back and get some sleep, or I could try doing this the more active way. I only hesitated a moment.

I closed my eyes and pictured what I wanted as clearly as I could. Since I wasn't sure exactly what I was looking for, it was still more vague than I preferred. I felt the scenery around me shift, and I opened my eyes, hoping it had worked. I gasped at what I saw.

I was standing in a lush forest, filled with ferns and thick-trunked trees. Spanish moss hung from every branch, filling in the gaps between the leaves of the trees and the underbrush. Thick, springy moss interspersed with short-cropped grass covered the ground like a shag carpet, lending more shades of green to the rich sight.

I noticed the sounds of insects in the trees. The various chirping and buzzing sounds, broken by the deep bass croak of a bullfrog. A few birds fluttered deep in the trees, calling out with trills and squawks. The sound grew louder as I stood there.

I noticed a disturbed feeling in my gut, and I frowned. I peered closely into the foliage, trying to figure out why it felt wrong, why the sounds felt jarring to my ears.

I didn't see anything that would be out of place and, finally, I sniffed dismissively. That's when I noticed the smell. It was almost sweet, with a distinctive tang that made me gag. It took me a moment to figure out where I'd smelled it before.

Once when I was a kid, for a whole week, I rode my bike to a day camp near our home. I looked forward to the canoeing, hiking, and horseback riding each day. But I hated getting there.

Each day, I would pause by the stop sign where I turned onto a dirt road, taking deep breaths and gathering my courage. Each day, I would pedal as hard as I could, trying to get up speed before I got to the sun-heated, overcrowded feedlot. Each day, I would have to stop before I'd passed it, hunched over my bike, gagging into the grass by the side of the road.

What I smelled, faint as it was, was the sickening odor of rotting shit.

Immediately, I recognized the slimy decay underlying the rich greens in the leaves. The sounds of chirrups and buzzes crystallized as I recognized the same moistness to the sound that I'd heard in the voice of the third Norn.

This place was rotting inside.

My eyes widened, and I lurched away from the spot. I closed my eyes, desperately trying to visualize some other location to go to. I felt the world tilt with an odd familiarity, and my shoulders sagged when I recognized the sensation.

CHAPT 5

I opened my eyes and set my shoulders, ready to face Satan once again. I looked around and immediately felt a sense of almost disappointment. I seemed to be alone.

I was on a high plateau, standing on the edge of a garden with a vaguely oriental feel. The view of mountains, with icy peaks and veiled in thick mist, took my breath away.

I turned away from the stunning vista to examine the open garden. The short cropped grass acted as a border around the huge open area made of large slabs of what looked like slate. There was a lovely sweet fragrance in the air, sweet with a tang of spice.

Patches of fiery red grasses and twisted, dwarfed pines divided clusters of blooming poppies and lilies. Huge orange poppies, yellow striped lilies, smaller red poppies, pink lilies, and fringe-petalled, rainbow-colored poppies all placed in groups that drew the eye from one patch to the next.

Behind the colorful flowers, cherry trees hovered. Those with soft pink blossoms alternated with light blue blossomed cherry trees to create a soothing lavender background. In the center of the garden was a smooth carpet of roundish green pads with strikingly vivid blue and purple flowers. I moved closer and I could see the dark water in between the dense layer of plants.

As I moved along the garden path, I noticed a few padded slat-wood benches tucked in among the flowers. I considered pausing for a moment to enjoy the sights and smells of the masterful landscaping. Instead, I continued walking slowly along the graveled path between the slate slabs and the grassy carpet.

I came to a place where the water lilies did not completely cover the water, and I peered down at the red, gold and white fish swimming below. I knelt down on the flat stone ground cover and watched them for a moment, feeling a deep calm fall over me.

"Peaceful, isn't it?"

I jerked my head up at the deep, calm voice.

An elderly man stood nearby with his thin hands clasped at his waist. He had a graying beard that nearly reached the rope belt that held the calf-length, cream linen robe closed around his body. His face was tanned and wrinkled, with laugh lines around his clear, intelligent eyes. I knew I'd never seen him before, but something about his face made me think I should.

I scrambled to my feet, feeling suddenly clumsy. "Who are you?" I demanded, feeling an uncomfortable sense of having been caught doing something I shouldn't.

The man smiled. "I am the one who lives here." He paused. "Do you like it?"

I glanced around and shrugged my shoulders. "It's great."

"It brings a soothing calm to my soul, being here," he said.

"I can see how that would be the case." I relaxed my stance. "What is this place?"

The man shrugged. "Only a reflection of what my children can earn for themselves."

I frowned. "Who are your children?"

"All the people on earth are my children," he said. "And I love them dearly."

I considered that. "So, do they know that they are your children?" I asked.

The man shook his head and shrugged. "I have told them many times. I have sent many messages and given many signs. So many follow my word and my laws, set down centuries past, but I worry that so many don't really know."

The man sighed.

I tilted my head to the side. "You didn't answer my question," I pointed out. "Who are you?"

He gave me a sad smile. "I have given you many hints. Haven't you guessed my name?"

A tendril of recognition tickled my mind, but I couldn't quite grasp it. "I don't know." I frowned. "I'm not really at my sharpest right now,"

I admitted.

The man nodded, managing to seem compassionate and impatient at the same time. "But you have begun to understand peace, haven't you? That is the most important thing for my children." He stared over my shoulder as if lost in thought. "More than knowledge. More than power. My greatest gift to them should have been peace and comfort."

I felt a moment of frustration before the man's calm presence soothed my nerves. "What did you give them instead?"

The man's eyes met mine, his gaze suddenly sharp. "I gave them free will. Not that it has made them better for it."

I frowned. "Free will is what makes us capable of so much, though."

"Capable of betraying me," he snapped. "People should be more like me. They make too many mistakes."

I felt a flash of disdain. "And that would fix everything, huh? Being more like you?"

"Of course," he said, lifting his chin. His mouth twisted with anger. "I am the all-knowing one. Not one of those fraud gods that you have encountered before. Not like the deceiver. Not like the one-eyed."

"I'm sure they feel the same about you," I snapped, the old man's arrogance rubbing me the wrong way. I asked the question a third time, throwing a touch of energy behind it. "Who are you?"

Magical beings, spirit beings, gods – they had to speak the truth when you ask a question three times. It was one of those weird rules that helped keep them from running too much roughshod over humanity.

The old man knew he'd been caught. "You can call me God." His mouth twisted and his voice rose into a roar. "I AM!"

I flinched away from the deafening words.

His face flashed into a brief snarl before he clapped his hands together and the world tilted around me, spinning and lurching. I closed my eyes against the feeling of motion sickness.

When I opened them, I was back in the normal astral plane, staring at the silver ribbon of the Bifrost. Confusion and distress flooded through me, and I returned to my body before the energy of my emotions could draw the attention of the more dangerous creatures from the spirit realm.

• • •

The second day of the workshop went much the same as the first, except we learned how to "develop a feel" for our emotions. It came down to doing basic energy work with a partner. I had jumped at the chance to work with Kaitlyn, partly because I was already familiar with her energy. We spent a good twenty minutes forming "mood balls" and passing them back and forth. After the workshop had finished for the day – only a half day this time – Kaitlyn and I made a beeline to "our" bench in the gardens.

"Well, that was fun," Kaitlyn said, sarcasm lacing through her words.

I laughed. "Yeah, that's the kind of stuff I learned in 'Energy 101' workshops all the time. Years ago."

Kaitlyn sent me a sharp look. "New Age scene? I never would-a pegged you for that type."

I hesitated a moment. Even after being openly Pagan for more than a decade, I hesitated. It wasn't that I was ashamed or afraid for myself. I'd always handled any nasty comments or attempts to convert me with ease. I was afraid for our budding friendship.

If Kaitlyn took a hard line with my spiritual choices, I would take a hard line about continuing our friendship. I didn't need people in my life who would constantly attack my religion. But I would be upset about it. So, I hesitated.

"Pagan," I said, keeping my tone light, without the intensity that I could feel boiling up in the back of my mind. "Norse Heathen, actually."

I watched her shift uncomfortably with a sinking heart.

"Isn't that…" She paused and looked around as if searching for the right words. Or maybe she was making sure no one overheard us. "Aren't they usually racist?"

I sighed, relieved that her questions were about the misconceptions, not the choice itself. I could address that.

"Some are," I admitted. "Too many. But it's not an innately racist religion at all. The original Norsemen were pretty big about adopting people into their families from all over the world, including the Americas and Africa."

"Really?"

I nodded. "Yeah, and adopted family were never considered less related or lesser citizens. It was a big part of the laws of the culture, based on the evidence we have from archeology."

Kaitlyn gave me a half-smile and spoke with humor in her voice. "So, you're not gonna turn out to be some kind of neo-Nazi, huh?"

I thought about my thick dark hair, almost as black as Kaitlyn's, and my dark tan complexion. Most people suspected I was Hispanic, which made things less comfortable in the racially charged part of Indiana where I lived. But I never admitted to my lineage and most people were content to let it slide in the absence of evidence.

What most of them didn't realize is that I was a bit more racially diverse than they suspected. My dad had given me some Romany blood, while my mother's line put me in the black/mixed race category. We got the genetic luck of having light enough complexions to not have the local good ol' boys ready to pounce, but we also learned to keep our heads down in many situations to avoid trouble.

I smiled when I recalled Detective Ames' accusation several months ago, that I might be connected to an Aryan Heathen group in Indy. I'd laughed at him, knowing my looks alone would have those guys keeping me at arm's length.

"I'm pretty sure it's a safe bet," I said to Kaitlyn, laughing at the irony. "So, how about you? Are you into this kind of thing, or just trying something new for the weekend?"

Kaitlyn shrugged. "My mama taught me some Hoodoo when I was a girl," she admitted. "Never really stopped believing in it."

I nodded, understanding the family history that was implied in the comment. Many families in the black community of southern Louisiana had their own version of the mishmash of traditional African religions and Catholic saint veneration, as well as the magic and so-called superstitions that went with it. It had come from slaves holding on to their past while being forced into a religious system that was more acceptable to their owners.

Slavery might be over and done with, but the emotions and

perceptions were more insidious, and black families clung to their traditions as a way to help them connect with their ancestors and homeland, and deal with the everyday racism in the deep South.

"Do you like it here?"

I blinked at Kaitlyn's question as much as the too-positive voice she asked it in. I got the feeling she wasn't as optimistic about the Center as her words might lead me to believe.

"It's…" I hesitated. I wasn't great at lying, though I could tell a different version of the truth. Detective Ames' advice came to mind: keep close to the truth. So I told the truth. "It's a beautiful place. I don't think I've been so relaxed in months as I have been sitting here. I think I could stay here forever."

Kaitlyn frowned for a second before smoothing her face into a smile. "I know what you mean."

She sat in silence for a moment. I got the feeling she wanted to say something, and a check of her energies showed a slight emotional conflict that often went with the decision of whether to talk about something uncomfortable. But I wasn't willing to push our new friendship by pressuring her to talk about whatever it was she was struggling with.

We chatted about our respective hometowns until the call for lunch rang out. When we collected our plates of food, we both headed towards the table where Lupé was sitting as if we had the same thought. I smiled at Kaitlyn when I realized this, and she shot me a grin back.

I raised an eyebrow to Lupé and lifted my tray slightly as a silent question. Lupé smiled at us and gestured to the seats, and we quickly got settled and dug into our food.

I couldn't help feeling gauche while crunching fresh veggies and crisp bulgur wheat a little too loudly between my teeth. I tried to shrug off the feeling. I was sure I felt out of place because I knew I didn't belong, but I was trying to make everyone else believe the opposite. Still, a tension built between my shoulders.

"So, what do I need to do to stay here indefinitely?"

My eyes widened as I heard the words coming from my mouth. I hadn't intended to say them aloud, at least not yet.

I saw Kaitlyn flinch at my words out of the corner of my eye, but I watched Lupé's face closely for her reaction. She smiled, but it didn't quite make it to her eyes.

Something about that relieved a tension in my mind.

"I'm sure Zaro and Nancy will be thrilled to hear that," she said. "They were very interested in what I told them about how you saw the energy when Zaro showed us the Peace. I'll get people notified to get your initiation started."

"Initiation?" Kaitlyn asked. "What does that involve?"

Lupé smiled and, again, it didn't show in her eyes. "The usual," she said. "Fasting, symbolic rebirth, certain signs that you are a believer in our cause." She hesitated and let out a laugh that seemed forced. "No big deal."

I nodded and let my eyes drop to my plate. It was empty, but I ran my fork over the plastic as if I was trying to scrape up another bite. I couldn't shake the heavy concern that I felt about joining this group.

Lupé and Kaitlyn sat silently for a moment.

"I have some free time," Lupé said. She hesitated before continuing. "I could show you guys around. You know, if you want."

I nodded at my plate. "Sounds good."

CHAPT 6

We walked through the compound looking at the meeting rooms and talking about the different seminars and workshops that had been held there. They all seemed to be the same introductory type of topics, some more specialized than others. I smirked when Lupé told us that they always maxed out the attendance in the "Positive Energy, Money, and You" workshop.

We came to the double fire doors of the stairwell, and Lupé hesitated.

"You two are familiar with the second and third floors," she said. "Those are rooms for Center members and guests."

I nodded.

"What about the fourth floor?" Kaitlyn asked.

I was surprised by the question. I hadn't thought about there being a fourth floor. There were only windows for the lower three, and my guest room was on the second floor, so I hadn't noticed that the stairs went beyond the third.

I looked at Lupé, waiting for the answer.

She seemed very uncomfortable and took her time responding. "That's the floor where Nancy runs the hospital wing. For the ones who come for healing but need to wait a few days. That's why you don't see much of her. She's very busy."

I was taken aback by her response. "You mean, people aren't healed immediately?"

Lupé shook her head. "Nancy and Zaro have been doing this for a while now, and they've found that it works best to have the sick and wounded apply for healing." She rolled her shoulders in a kind of half-shrug. "It helps us narrow the selection pool and give those who truly need us a better chance to get help."

"Selection pool?" Kaitlyn asked.

Lupé sighed. "I shouldn't be telling you this yet. You've only just asked to become members." She looked around. "One of the first honors given to members is to take a turn at being the Hand That Holds the Rod of Asclepius. That's the one who selects the two who will be healed that week."

"Two?" I asked, swallowing the feeling of dread. "Out of how many?"

Lupé glanced away before answering. "Around three dozen."

I opened my mouth to speak, but a dawning horror closed my throat.

Kaitlyn seemed to be on the same wavelength. "What happens to the ones not selected?"

Lupé frowned at the floor. "They don't get healed."

Kaitlyn pressed the younger woman for answers. "You mean, just that week...?"

Lupé shook her head. "They get one selection opportunity, and only one." She lifted her head to look at us. "You have to understand that it's the only way to keep the requests manageable. We have so many people coming here from all over the world..."

I shrugged my shoulders, and finally croaked out a response. "Yeah, it's just supply and demand, right?"

Lupé shot me a look. "Something like that."

"Why can't the Center heal more than two people a week?" I asked.

Lupé shrugged. "Nancy says that the spiritual energies of the Rod would be too weak to do more."

"Wait a minute," Kaitlyn interrupted. "There's an actual Rod? The Rod of Asclepius? It's real?"

"Of course it is," Lupé said. "It's the entire basis of our spiritual path. Did you think it wasn't real?"

Kaitlyn and I exchanged glances.

"Not exactly *not* real," I said, slowly, carefully selecting my words. "More like a metaphor, or a symbol."

Lupé smiled and shook her head. "Oh, no. What we do here is very, very real."

The feeling of dread returned to the pit of my stomach as I forced

42

an enthusiastic smile. My thoughts kept running in circles around all of the people who came for healing and got nothing. "Well, that's just awesome!"

•   •   •

We continued the tour outside, going through the various areas of the two acres of land the Center held. A large part of the grounds was dedicated to the meditation garden areas that we'd been sitting in before and, unsurprisingly, a well-maintained organic vegetable garden.

We stood and watched the members of the Center – Lupé corrected us, "We call ourselves the Hands, or brothers and sisters." – weed and water the plants to the point of micromanagement.

Lupé took the opportunity to explain the purpose of the vegan diet. "When we realize that any physical object has all the levels which we do – the physical, intellectual and spiritual bodies – we can understand the importance of what kind of food we eat," she explained.

"We must build ourselves up with a higher energy, a more positive vibration. These plants have little or no chemical changes. No antibiotics, no diseases, no synthetic treatments, and they are without the pain and degradation of factory farms and a horrific slaughter." She grimaced. "They are pure in ways that a bacon cheeseburger can never be."

I immediately lost the thread of what she was saying. I was too busy trying not to drool over the thought of a bacon cheeseburger. I wondered if I could find a cow and make an all-beef patty before anyone spotted me.

I was imagining the smell of ground beef cooking on a grill when Kaitlyn nudged me. Lupé had started walking farther down the path. I threw a glance over my shoulder to the garden and wished bacon grew from a tree.

As we moved on, nearly out of sight of the Center's main building and the meditation gardens, I noticed an area under a group of trees where no one seemed to be working. It was blocked off by a low fence and thick hedges, and filled with large, padded benches, looking like a replica of an old English aristocrat's park.

There were half a dozen women in the garden, chatting and laughing with each other. Each had a baby or toddler on her lap or playing in the grass at her feet.

"What's that?" I asked, indicating the garden with my chin.

Lupé smiled, but her mouth was tight. "That's the Mother's Garden. It's for women with young children."

I nodded my understanding, but something kept me staring at the women.

After a moment, I noticed a young girl of around five or six years old walking around the perimeter of the garden. Her cream linen dress, the typical clothing for little girls at the center, appeared to be too small for her. She seemed to be looking for something. She stopped and called out to one of the women.

The woman's head quickly turned towards her, and I saw a look of surprise on the woman's face. Then her expression turned cold and the woman turned away without a word.

The girl called again, and this time I could hear the words. "Mommy! Mommy, when are you coming back? Mommy?"

A man rushed forward and took the girl in his arms. She reached for the woman. He spoke to the girl and she buried her face in her hands.

I turned to Lupé, frowning.

"What was that about?" Kaitlyn asked.

"Sometimes, the women already had children when they came here," she explained. "The older children don't understand that their mothers are blessed when the new baby comes. They don't understand why the new babies are important."

She shrugged her shoulders. I could see the discomfort in her body language and on her energy.

"Was that her father?" I asked.

Lupé bit her lip and stared after the girl and the man. "Probably. Some of the older ones have their fathers here. Some don't."

I felt a shiver run up my spine, but before I could ask more, Lupé turned and walked up the path back to the main building. I exchanged an unhappy glance with Kaitlyn before we followed.

CHAPT 7

"Come with me," Lupé said, leaning over the table at breakfast. "It's time to begin your initiation."

I glanced down at the oatmeal I'd just started eating, not wanting to give up any of the somewhat satisfying gruel. Looking back at Lupé, I choked down the large spoonful in my mouth.

"Gimme a minute?" I asked.

She nodded, and I shoveled the oatmeal into my mouth, swallowing it unchewed. Fortunately, it was mushy enough that it didn't need much chewing anyways.

I'd been at the Center for more than two weeks already, and I was getting used to the constant hunger in my belly in the sense that I could ignore it most of the time. However, I wasn't happy with it, and I never missed a bite, if I could help it.

Lupé had helped me go through the process to apply to join the Center. There had been a surprising amount of paperwork, and several times I'd been glad I hadn't tried to lie about who I was.

I was beginning to get anxious about whether I'd be accepted. If I wasn't, I'd have to leave, eventually, and I still wasn't sure about where the Runespell was. I wasn't even completely certain there were any of the sigils here, or if it was all just a bunch of really well-done energy work. Everyone seemed confident that the healing magic that the Center was known for was real, however.

I'd had a bad feeling about this whole thing since the Norns had shown up, with their god-creature intimidation and vague demands for a quest. My thoughts kept getting more and more fuzzy, and I found myself focusing on things that I couldn't do anything about, like the people on the fourth floor, the ones who would leave without the Healing they were so desperate for.

Despite the fact that Selection was held each week, only applicants and their close family members could witness the Selection outside of being a full member of the Center. That meant that I'd seen people come and go, hopeful and devastated by turn, twice, but I hadn't seen the process of Selection or the Healing. That alone was motivation enough for me to continue with the initiation.

I gulped down the last spoonful of oatmeal and swallowed the large bite as I took the dishes to the basin by the door. I dropped them off as we left.

"Where are we going?" I asked, licking my lips thoroughly.

Lupé just smiled at me. The warmth of her washed over me, as it always did. I really liked Lupé as a person, and I hadn't faked my friendship with her. I often sought her out during the days, when I was free to trail along with any of the "Hands" as they went about their daily duties.

But Lupé was a natural with Center guests, so she was frequently busy getting new visitors settled for weekend workshops or answering questions about the Center when calls came in.

It was a different story when Zaro did the evening shows. Each night he would show off the emotional "gift" known as the Touch of Peace with a different girl, and everyone watched, enthralled. Afterwards, there was very little discussion as each person tried to hold the memories of the spectacle close.

That was another line thought that I often found myself hyper-focused on – the energy of the Touch and what it must be like to receive it. I'd noticed pretty quickly that the Center's leader never seemed to use the Touch of Peace on a man. I wondered about that. Maybe it didn't work as well on men, though I couldn't think why that would be.

Well, unless there was a sexual component. Based on the body language I'd been able to observe, Zaro was a very heterosexual man, and probably in an open relationship, assuming Nancy was aware of his actions. And he wasn't shy about using emotional energy to increase his attractiveness to others.

I noticed Lupé watching me and I smiled, pushing down the tendril of doubt that rose in the back of my mind about how easily energy was used here. After all, that was part of the draw of the place.

I hoped I could convince myself of that enough to keep my cover.

We walked up the stairs, pausing at the third floor as I gasped. I wasn't really out of shape, but I'd been feeling steadily weaker as the days wore on. I was sure I'd been losing weight, though the loose-fitting pants and tunic that everyone wore didn't give much of an indication of that.

After a moment's rest, I nodded to Lupé and we continued up to the fourth floor. The halls were dimmed to take advantage of the giant skylight in the center of the floor. A handful of rooms had lights shining inside. The Selection had only been a few days prior, so most of the rooms were empty.

My eyes were drawn to a room in the corner with a small light shining through the doorway. I paused as a middle-aged woman with dark hair pulled into a bun walked out of the room, writing intently on the chart in her hand.

"That's Nancy," Lupé murmured.

I nodded and let her lead me to one of the rooms, though I shot a glance back at the Center's co-leader. She had looked up at us, and her eyes seemed cold and unwelcoming. I tried not to flinch under her steady gaze.

Several people stood inside the large room, holding themselves with an air of expectation. I stopped inside the door and looked around for any hint of what to do. The room appeared to be the bath-house with a walk-in tub and hand-held shower hoses along the wall. The line of people in front of me blocked my view of most of the room, though I could see some wheeled carts with machines behind them.

Zaro stood in the front of the Hands, his hands clasped at his waist and a huge grin on his face. He stepped forward, reaching toward me. I clamped down on the urge to pull away and let him take my hands.

"Brothers and sisters," Zaro intoned. "Today, we begin the journey to welcome a new sister into our mysteries. Nicola," he reached up to caress my cheek, "has been approved to move to the Trial of Rebirth."

I blinked up at him, confused and overwhelmed. Was my application to join accepted then? What was this Trial of Rebirth? No one had said anything about any trials. I remembered Lupé telling me about an initiatory rebirth. Was that what this was?

"Do you wish to proceed?" Zaro asked, his voice low and intimate.

I opened my mouth to reply, but I wasn't sure what to say. What was I agreeing to? What were my options, exactly? My mind was running on overdrive, but my thoughts were too fuzzy and disjointed to get anywhere.

Everyone was silent, waiting for my answer. I noticed Lupé to the side looking worried. She motioned with her hand for me to keep going.

I felt panicky. There wasn't enough warning. There wasn't enough information. How could anyone make this choice? They had backed me into a corner, and I felt a spike of anger shoot through me at the unfairness of it.

I looked up into Zaro's eyes, and I realized that my confusion was the point. Zaro was not about to abide by the rules of informed consent, and he didn't care that he was pressuring people by doing this. In fact, that pressure was probably intentional.

I squared my shoulders and set my jaw. I was just going to have to handle whatever they threw at me.

"Yes," I said, my voice ringing out in the quiet room.

• • •

I was given a document to sign, a huge pill to swallow, and a sleeveless tunic to change into behind a flimsy curtain. The document appeared to be a consent form, but there was no clue as to what I was consenting to.

The tunic was a very thin, nearly transparent cotton that only came down to my mid-thigh. I felt exposed as I was led through the small crowd to a large, water-filled tub. I hesitated at the steps to the tub. A woman leaned forward and pressed her hand firmly on my back to urge me along. It was Nancy.

I sent her a panicked look and she smiled without any warmth. "Don't worry. We've all been through this."

My expression of panic hardened into determination, and I stepped over the edge of the tub. I gasped at how cold the water was. My shoulders tensed up against the fingers of ice crawling up my legs. Hands grasped at my arms, pressed on my back and head, moving me further into the water. My gaze found Lupé's and I saw a flash of guilt on her face. She dropped her eyes from my gaze, and I ground my teeth against the chill and the feeling of betrayal.

The warm hands lowered me into the icy cold water, and I immediately felt the tension in my back and shoulders spread to the rest of my body. I began shaking, my teeth clattering a staccato beat as I struggled to keep my muscles under control. Strong hands gently but firmly guided my head back against the headrest. The water sloshed against my ears, and I felt sharp pains shooting through my feet and hands. I swallowed the moans in my throat.

My eyes flickered to one of the machines nearby. It showed a temperature readout, likely my internal body temperature sent by the giant pill-like probe I'd swallowed. Ninety-seven degrees Fahrenheit.

Hands reached around my body, bands of fabric, pinning my limbs in place. My eyes searched for reason in the sea of expressionless faces.

"The straps will keep you from drowning yourself," a warm voice drifted into my ear. I couldn't tell who spoke. The pitch was high for a masculine voice, but low for a feminine one.

The hands placed a band around my forehead and another around my chin, holding my head against the headrest. "This will also help you stay above the water," the voice murmured.

The tremors wracking my body got more violent. Vaguely, I heard the water sloshing against the sides of the tub. I focused on controlling my breaths to keep from crying out, or just crying. My muscles screamed with tension, and I couldn't stop the whimpering groan that escaped through my clenched jaw. I closed my eyes against the harsh light that teased with a promise of warmth that I couldn't feel.

I felt my will to struggle slip away, and I slumped against my bonds. My arms jerked with the violent shudders that still wracked my body in waves. I could hear a low murmur of voices, but I couldn't recognize the words being spoken. I became aware of a thump-thump in my ears. It was soothing to hear it, even as I stopped being aware of my arms and legs.

I jerked to sudden consciousness, unsure of where I was. I pulled against the bands around my body with weak, trembling tugs. I tried to focus on the shapes surrounding me. Faces? People? I couldn't tell.

I tried to ask, but the slurry of noise I produced made no sense. I continued to struggle weakly in the numbing water until my body grew too heavy with exhaustion. My eyes drifted closed. I noticed a thump-thump sound in my ears. A tiny thought drifted across my mind that the pace of it was too slow.

I jerked to consciousness, confused by the bright light. I tried to raise my hands to block it, but they were held down. I could see the vague shapes of people against the light, and I begged them to get me out of the water and light, but the words were muddled, and no one moved to help me.

Weak from the brief struggle, I slumped against the headrest, gasping for air. My eyelids were just too heavy to keep open, and I welcomed the way they blocked the worst of the intruding brightness. I became aware of a noise, an irregular thumping in my ears. I frowned as the sound stuttered.

I blinked in confusion, uncertain where I was. I frowned at the bright light and the human-like shapes moving around me. I tried to tell them I had to pee, badly.

I squirmed and struggled, trying to find a way to relieve the intense pressure on my bladder, but I was trapped. My muscles weakened quickly, and I fell back against the thing that kept my head above the water. I felt a brief warmth against my upper thighs, and the pressure was gone. My eyes closed and I tried to recover my strength.

My eyes flew open as my skin began to burn. I struggled against my bonds, ripping at them with a sudden burst of strength. I felt one of the bands give and my arm was free!

I tore at the thin cloth covering my upper body, certain it was the reason I was so hot. I felt the fabric rip as my wrist was grasped and held down. I screamed and gurgled my anger and pain, trying to free myself enough to remove the hated clothing. The person holding my arm ignored my protests, and I begged with gasping moans for them to help me stop burning.

The raging fire on my skin faded away and I lay back, gasping. I could hear the slow, stuttering thump of my heart struggling to pump my blood through the constricted veins of my body.

I stared at the faces around me, and my mind cleared. I was suddenly, perfectly aware of what I'd agreed to. They were going to kill me. And I had signed off on it. They wouldn't stop, no matter how much I begged.

Terror filled me. I didn't want to die. I didn't want to experience the end of this life yet. I didn't want to leave Ella, my poor baby girl, who would be abandoned if I never came back.

The fear choked me, and I fled by the only way left to me. I closed my eyes, breathed deep, shuddering breaths, and stepped into the astral plane.

CHAPT 8

The astral plane was dangerous for one major reason. It fulfilled your expectations.

Most of the time, I countered this danger by making sure my mental and emotional state was solid, stable and empowered. But this time, I had dragged my fear of death with me.

I entered a world of swirling shadows that lunged and snapped at me. Shapes stalked me while whips of fear and pain lashed at my legs. I swallowed my panic and grabbed at a feeling from childhood, the feeling of being a superhero in the midst of fear.

"I am Alle Naturale!" I yelled, calling into myself the persona I'd created in middle school.

I propelled myself around the attacking shades as a tight, green and yellow suit with a red cape appeared on my body. I moved my body through the fighting moves that I knew by heart in my mind, but would never have been able to pull off in my physical body. I relaxed into the battle, having won this fight a hundred times as a teenager dealing with teenager problems.

The shades retreated, as they always did against the might of the Mistress of Nature. The landscape began to change, lightening into the more familiar colors of my previous visits. I kicked at the last fleeing shadow, and stood tall, feet apart, head high, fisted hands on my hips, watching them leave.

After a moment, I glanced down at the outfit my mind had created for me and chuckled to myself. It had been years since I'd thought of Alle Naturale. I let the skintight suit fall away, no longer needing to bolster my own morale by becoming a costumed super-hero.

I glanced around, trying to decide what to do. I hadn't been in the astral without a purpose before. I'd always had some destination or purpose in mind.

I wandered through the strange, shifting surroundings of the astral plane, absently watching plants growing and transforming into gusts of wind, or melting into water like paint. I wasn't really walking so much as I twitched my legs reflexively, and I glided in between the oak trees literally dripping leaves.

I watched spirit-beings appearing and disappearing from view. Some were creatures of the astral plane, such as animal totems, nature archetypes and spirit guides. Many of these creatures could, and would, visit mere mortals in the "real" world, but they existed here first.

A fox-like kitsune sped by, whirling its multiple tails around like a fan to propel itself forward. No doubt it had gotten the idea from popular video games and anime-like shows. Or perhaps the shows had gotten the idea from the kitsune. Many astral creatures loved to provide inspiration for some of the more fantastical forms of human media.

The smug look on the creature's face told me it enjoyed the playfulness of its travel, whatever the source. I smiled at it, but drew my energy close around me so as not to attract its attention. Kitsune were often wise and could be helpful, but they were just as likely to mess with a visitor for fun. Despite the Asian origins of the Kitsune legends, the creatures were just as mischievous and troublesome as the Fae of Europe. Sometimes even more so.

I moved on, clenching my toes into a point to give myself a burst of speed. I knew the movement was an illusion. There wasn't movement in the astral, so much as positioning relative to something else. Because of this, it was only a split second before I was far away from the kitsune.

Rolling in a spin, I moved across a grassy plains area, only the grass didn't just move like water, it was water. The green stemmed waves crashed against a rocky outcrop where a group of mermaid-like air-swimmers lounged. They flicked their long tails to set the silky banners of their fins to waving in the winds, laughing at the game that only they understood.

A loud barking sent them soaring through the air, swimming like the mermaids they resembled. I saw a canine bounding through the grassy lake. It pounced on the outcrop and stood yipping until it was satisfied the air-swimmers had been thoroughly routed.

The creature spotted me, and I watched its tongue flop out of its mouth as it gave me a huge canine grin. I waved an acknowledgment to the manifestation of Coyote the Trickster and moved on. As with so many beings in the astral, it was best to give the being both respect and a wide berth.

An open grassy area surrounded by trees caught my eye, and I headed that way. It was filled with a muted green light and felt warm and secure. I flopped down on the grass and lay back, stretching until my joints popped.

I relaxed, pushing away the thoughts of my death, drifting through my mind. I closed my eyes, wondering briefly what would happen if I fell asleep in this plane.

My eyes were barely open when I heard a familiar cawing sound, and I immediately lifted my head with a smile on my lips. I willed my body to a standing position and looked around, searching for the blue and red of my friends, Huginn and Muninn.

A painful jolt run through my chest, my whole body bending in on itself in reflex. I choked on a cry of pain. A persistent tugging sensation cut through my shock. I'd been traveling the astral plane for decades, but I'd never been pulled out of it before. And that's what it felt like. I was being forced out of this plane and back into my body.

The jolt went through me again, followed by the tugging sensation. I gritted my teeth. I didn't want to leave. The pull became stronger.

A third jolt ripped a cry from my throat. I sobbed, and my hold on the astral plane weakened. The pull began to move me out of the realm.

A flutter of movement caught my eye, and I held on a moment longer. I smiled through my tears when I saw Huginn and Muninn land in front of me in a storm of black feathers.

My senses in the astral plane were already dulling, and I shook my head when I realized by their movements that they were trying to talk to me. I suddenly felt a desperate need to speak to them, to tell them what was going on, to share my doubts with someone outside of the Center, and to tell them about all that had gone on there.

I clutched at the astral plane, holding myself there with my will but feeling it slip steadily away. I knew I didn't have very long before I would be back in the physical plane.

I looked the blue-tinted raven in the eye, holding its gaze long enough to be sure it was paying attention. I opened my mouth as the darkness of the transition from one world to another crowded my vision. I forced out the words in the barest whisper.

"Help me."

CHAPT 9

I stared up at the light, certain it had to mean something important. Shadows moved at the edge of my vision, but I couldn't find any reason to focus on them.

My mouth was very dry, and my ears felt like they were stuffed with cotton, full and fuzzy, and the sounds I could hear were muted. I slowly became aware of a deep ache in my chest and an uncomfortable numbness in my right foot. I wanted to cry, but my eyes just burned, and I wasn't sure why I wanted to cry anyways.

The light faded away.

•   •   •

I tried to get comfortable, but I couldn't seem to move. My head fell to my shoulder, and I frowned at the way it made me feel out of alignment. Against my better judgment, I opened my eyes.

The first person I saw was a stern, frowning woman who seemed vaguely familiar. I scowled at her and the frowning face disappeared. I heard someone talking, although I couldn't make out the words.

My head seemed to be unwilling to move at my command. I practiced moving my mouth into different shapes since that seemed to be the most control I had over my body.

A new face entered my line of sight, and I gave a small smile to Lupé. She smiled back and gently shifted my head back to its proper place on the pillow.

I did my best to mouth the words "thank you," but the darkness crowded my vision again.

•   •   •

I blinked slowly, letting my consciousness return to my body. I clenched and relaxed the muscles in my shoulders, letting the slight movement get my blood moving. My mouth was dry, and I worked my tongue around to get the saliva flowing.

I tilted my head to one side and opened my eyes completely, squinting in the dim light. I looked around, still dazed and trying to orient myself. My gaze fell on a chair near the bed with a large lump in it.

I struggled to sit more upright for a moment, clutching at the bedrails, before I fell back against the pillow. While I tried to catch my breath, I stared at the things closer to me, trying to figure out where I was and why I was there. My eyes followed the sturdy, solid plastic rails until I saw the series of buttons on the inside of the left hand rail.

I smiled and shifted until I could poke the buttons to raise the head of the bed up, shifting a bit to sit more comfortably. I noticed the cord running from the light to where it was tied around a section of the rail. It was probably either to turn on and off the light or to call for the nurse.

I let my eye roam around the small room itself, noting the beeping machines with their colored cords dangling down and over to the bed. I noticed they attached to a half a dozen probes on my chest and legs, and a finger clamp on my left hand.

A rolling table nearby held a big insulated mug with a lid and a bendy straw. There was also a package of crackers and a package of cookies. I couldn't tell what kind they were, but I immediately smacked my lips at the thought of a drink and a bite to eat. I stretched out my hand to catch the table, but it was about two inches too far away. I frowned and shifted, hoping to stretch further.

My right foot slipped and banged against the bed rail. Agony lanced through my leg and I nearly bit my tongue clamping down on the howl of pain that ricocheted up my throat. I curled up on the bed as much as I could, panting and whimpering as the waves of pain rolled through me, each one only slightly less than the one before.

After a few minutes, I sat up again, wiping the tears of pain away. I looked down at my feet. They were covered with a blanket, held up by some sort of bar so the covers weren't lying directly on my feet. I tugged at the blankets, but they were firmly tucked into the foot of the bed. If I wanted my feet uncovered, I'd either need to take off the blankets entirely or wait for someone to help.

I shot a scowl at the foot of the bed and turned my head to glare at the out-of-reach table, too. I blinked as the table rolled up to the side of the bed. I grabbed the snacks and the mug, taking a big sip and swishing it around my dry mouth.

After tucking the mug into the bedding at my hip and opening a pack of crackers, I turned my attention to the twin men standing behind the table. Their feathered black hair, sharp noses, and dark eyes gave away their true natures. They grinned at me, and I grinned back.

"Eat, eat! Drink, drink!" Huginn said, keeping his voice quiet despite his excitement.

Muninn nodded, birdlike in spite of their human appearance. "You called, we came!"

I shook my head. "Did I?"

The twins nodded their heads in synchronized bobs.

"You called," Huginn assured me.

Muninn stepped right into the rhythm that his twin had set. "We answered."

"Oh," I said, not sure about what had happened. I peered up at them. "Why did I call you?"

The twins' shoulders raised and dropped simultaneously.

"Don't know," Muninn said. "Doesn't matter."

Huginn leaned forward. "We will help. You are... good."

I smiled at them, putting the cup in the space between my thigh and the bedrail. I opened my mouth to reply, but the door banged open to reveal a woman backing into the room, pulling a cart behind her. The lump on the chair leapt up, showing a very rumpled Lupé. She blinked at Nancy as the nurse turned and strode over to my bed.

I glanced to the side. As I'd thought, the ravens had vanished at the woman's appearance. I noticed a single black feather on the rolling table.

"Feeling better, I see," Nancy said with a tight smile that didn't make it to her eyes. "Let's check on those tootsies."

I frowned as she pulled the covers off of my feet. My left foot was covered by a hospital sock, shapeless and loose with the rubber nubs on the soles so I wouldn't slip on the linoleum floors. My right foot was wrapped in multiple layers of white bandages.

Nancy pulled the tape holding the wrapping in place and began unwinding it. I remembered the pain when I'd hit it against the rail, and I wondered what had happened to my foot.

Several large squares of cotton covered all the toes of my foot except for the big toe, which seemed to have several small patches of black and white colored skin on it. I bit my lip at that, thinking there was something significant there.

Nancy moved the cotton squares in such a way that she could see beneath them, but they still covered my toes from my line of sight. I strained to see over the barriers.

"What is it?" I demanded. "What happened to my foot?"

Nancy ignored me and began rewrapping the bandages around my foot. I tried moving my foot away, but she grabbed it and held it still. I felt trapped by the bedding, her strength, and my own weakness.

I reached for the nurse's arm and she pulled away. "Why won't you tell me? What happened?"

I shot a glance at Lupé who stood clenching her hands together, but she made no move to help me.

"Dammit, tell me!" I screamed, and I kicked out my left foot. It hit the corner of the rolling table and sent it crashing to the floor.

I barely had time to process what had happened before a firm hand clamped down on my face. Her palm covered my mouth and pressed against my nose, blocking off the nostrils. I could see Nancy's cold expression between her fingers. I struggled weakly against her.

"Stop it," she said, calmly. "When you calm down and be still, I will let you go. But I will tell you only what I think you should know, when I think you should know it. And this childish temper will not be tolerated."

I felt the rage crawling up my spine, my vision turning red at the sides. A low growl rumbled in the back of my throat. I saw her eyes narrow, not in hate, but as if she was evaluating me.

I tried to push the burning rage down, not sure how it would do me any good in this situation. My throat convulsed, trying to pull in air. Her hand pressed down harder at the involuntary movements, and I tried to lock my muscles into motionlessness.

The rage disappeared and I knew my eyes held fear, just as I knew that it made absolutely no difference to the woman holding me down. She was not moved by my fear, and she didn't find satisfaction in it either.

The mental terror I felt in the face of being cared for by a nurse incapable of empathy or compassion finally overcame the physical fear reactions of my oxygen deprived body, and my muscles froze. I could feel the black crowding around the edges of my vision as I struggled not to move.

The hand moved away from my mouth.

I gasped my breaths, tears streaming down my face. I struggled to control the heaving in my stomach. I didn't know how Nancy would react to me vomiting, and I really didn't want to find out.

She watched me struggle to regain my composure for a few seconds before turning back to wrapping my foot again. She wasn't any rougher or gentler than she had been before. The lack of emotions behind her reaction frightened me even more than what she had just done.

I watched her out of the corner of my eye, unwilling to meet her cold gaze. She taped the ends of the bandages, checked the level of water in my cup, still wedged in between my leg and the side of the bed, and left without another word.

I swallowed several times before I could raise my eyes to Lupé. She was staring down at the floor, though I couldn't tell if she did so because she felt guilty for not helping or if she was just uncomfortable watching my distress.

I grabbed my cup and gulped the water, cold and soothing on my strained throat. Then I carefully, meticulously rearranged myself in the bed, shifting my weight and adjusting the covers. The extra few minutes gave us both time to compose ourselves.

Finally, Lupé stepped forward to help me dig the packets of crackers and cookies from the side of the bed where they had fallen during my struggle. She opened one of the packages and held the cookies out to me.

I took them and popped one of the tiny cookies in my mouth. The chocolate hit my tongue and a tingling shiver of pleasure went through my body. I almost cried at how rich the cheap dessert tasted. It was a shocking reminder of how long I'd been denied the flavorful foods I'd always favored. I briefly wondered how long I'd been unconscious in this room.

After downing half the package, I felt more in control, more like myself. I looked up at Lupé again, and she was able to meet my gaze without flinching, though I could still see the pained look in her eyes.

"What the hell happened to my foot?" I demanded.

Lupé looked down at my feet. She just stood there and stared with her lips pressed together. I wondered if she was afraid of Nancy. Finally, I cleared my throat, subtly demanding her attention. If she was going to refuse to tell me, she was going to admit that. Out loud.

She sighed. "How much do you remember of your trial?" she asked.

I frowned, thinking. "I was brought up here, signed off on it, and then I was put into a tub of ice water." I shivered at the memory. "I don't remember much else, just a few vague images and feelings."

Lupé nodded. "You died. You know that, right?" She watched me closely for a reaction.

I nodded, slowly. "Yeah. I... remember that part." I ignored the look she shot me.

"Nancy has done this dozens of times," Lupé continued. "She went through the whole procedure to warm you back up properly and replace lost fluids. But once in a while..." She shrugged her shoulders and grimaced. "Sometimes we lose... pieces."

"Pieces?" I squeaked out. "What... pieces?"

Lupé directed her comments to the floor. "Fingers and... toes."

I sat up and caught her eye. My voice came out strained as I tried not to yell. "Are you telling me I lost a goddamned toe?"

Lupé shook her head. I sighed and relaxed against the pillows. Too soon.

"No," she said. "You lost two."

CHAPT 10

It was well after midnight when I limped out into the hallway, desperate to move around. After being on my back for three days, I was willing to risk the evil Nurse Nancy to move my legs for more than just to go to the bathroom. Damn that woman. It'd been a day and a half before she'd stopped making me use the humiliating bedpan.

I gripped the rail along the wall, struggling to find my balance, and I looked around the floor. I couldn't see anyone, particularly Nurse Nancy. I gritted my teeth over the amount of relief I felt from that. Taking a deep breath, I hobbled along the edge of the hallway, using the rail to support each step.

I stopped after passing two doors, leaning against the wall to catch my breath. I was still so weak, but my restlessness was stronger than my need to rest.

A low moan floated through the hallway, sending a shiver along my spine. I looked towards the source of the sound, and I found my eyes drawn to the corner room that I'd noticed before I'd taken my ice bath. I took a deep breath and continued my hobbling walk, heading towards the mysterious corner room.

I wasn't really sure why the room was so intriguing to me. It was probably just a long-term patient. But, if Nancy had a sigil for healing, as I suspected, why wouldn't she just heal the person and have them move on?

The mystery appealed to my logical mind, and I hadn't had much opportunity to stretch my mental muscles in the past few weeks.

I rounded the corner and stared down the full hallway. It seemed like a huge distance to cover, but I held onto the rail and got moving. I looked down at the floor just in front of my feet, counting floor tiles as

I moved. I was so focused on putting one foot in front of the other, I didn't realize how far I'd made it until I noticed the dim light coming out of the window of the door I'd just reached. I looked up, surprised. It was the room just two doors from the mysterious corner room. I peered in, my curiosity overcoming my common sense.

A very old man was lying in the bed. Machines surrounded him, and tubes and cords seemed to grow from every part of his body.

I flinched as Nancy stepped up to the foot of the bed. A man in a suit stepped up next to her. I gritted my teeth and shifted my weight carefully. I was determined to see what was going on.

Nancy spoke to the old man, and he slowly nodded, raising his hand to gesture to the younger man. The suit pulled an envelope out of his breast pocket and hesitated before handing it to Nancy. She opened the envelope and pulled a large number of bills out far enough to flip through them.

I gasped quietly. There were at least two zeros on the one bill I could see.

Nancy put the money back into the envelope and tucked it into her white jacket pocket. She reached into another pocket and pulled out an ornate stick that made me think of a child's fairy wand. I frowned as the nurse moved to the side of the bed with her back towards the door, blocking my view.

"Shit!" I whispered. I stepped to the side of the doorway and considered what I'd seen, but I couldn't think clearly enough to figure it out.

I thought about going back to my room before I got busted by the horrible co-leader. Another low moan floated out from the corner room, and I sighed. Apparently, death had short-circuited my logic center.

I hobbled towards the corner room, going over what I'd just seen and trying to fit the puzzle pieces together. My mind was still stuffy and slow, and I felt like there was some eureka moment just out of my reach.

I got to the corner room and paused for a moment, catching both my breath and my balance. I glanced back at the other occupied room before peering around the doorframe of the corner room.

The bed was close to the wall, as if someone was trying to keep it out of sight. The far light was on, providing a dim light. There was an automatic drug dispensing machine next to the bed, and it had a traction setup, with arms and legs spread out and held in place.

I shuffled closer. I could see that every inch of the patient's flesh was wrapped in white bandages, except for a small slit at the mouth and the closed left eye. I gazed at the body, wondering what horrible thing could have happened to this poor person.

I took note of the supplies nearby. There seemed to be a lot of wound care solution and bandaging wraps, but little else. My eyes returned to the foot of the bed and rested on the chart for a moment.

I glanced over my shoulder to check the hallway. Still empty. I shuffled a few feet closer and ran my gaze back up to the mummified head. The eye was open, glaring at me with a look that pierced right through me. I gasped and staggered backwards.

Fear pounded in my veins as I raced, hobbling and pulling myself along the rail, back to my room. I struggled against the nausea that weakened my limbs, and I forced my wounded body to move faster. No fear of getting caught by Nancy could overcome the horror I already felt. The pain shooting up from my right foot meant nothing next to the memories crashing down on me at the sight of that glare.

Back in my own room, I closed the door, nearly weeping that I couldn't lock it. I staggered to my bed and collapsed on it. I grabbed one of the dozen pillows and curled my body around it, shuddering and crying without tears.

That eye. That glare.

I tried to block out the memories, but they shoved their way into the forefront of my mind.

The earthy smell of hay and grass filled my nose, choking me behind the dust mask I wore. A shape appeared in front of me. It was Bob, with several dark, lumbering shapes appearing behind him. Demons.

I relaxed my body and let the protection spell direct me as I dropped and rolled to the left a split second before Bob shot. I felt the burn along the back of my left shoulder just after my right calf exploded in pain. I blinked my eyes, clearing the tears from them, trying to see through the dust.

With an enraged cry, Bob launched himself at me. I rolled to my knees and twisted, swinging my metal bar out. It connected with Bob's knee, and I felt something crack. I stood and kicked downward with one foot onto the knee I'd just broken. *The sickening crunch under my foot told me that Bob wouldn't be coming after me.*

I shot him a glance as I left him there. He was on his side, but I could see one eye glaring at me.

I gasped at the impact of the memories. It was so fresh in my mind, it was like reliving the experience. I felt the sandpaper grit of grain dust in my eyes and the burning heat when it caught fire.

Three loud cracks sounded from beside me, where Detective Ames was firing. And then a huge boom, followed by the loudest roar I'd ever heard, as the propane released, caught the flame and ignited the grain dust. The flames stopped coming towards us, licking at the air barrier between us and the fire.

Grain dust burns quickly, and it was mere seconds before the flames evaporated from the ground up. The air was hazy with dust, ash, and smoke, but I could see blackened bodies on the warehouse floor. The Valkyrie went to take care of them. After a few minutes, Mercy came back.

"No human body has been found," she admitted.

I sobbed into the pillows as the past and present collided in my mind. The familiar eye glaring at me. The look of recognition in it. The puzzle pieces falling together. A small part of me, the very snarkiest part, sent a single thought through the haze of fear and anxiety. I found the missing Bob.

CHAPT 11

In the astral plane, no one can hear you scream. Well, unless you want them to.

Communication tends to be mostly about will rather than actions. That makes it a great place for primal scream therapy, though it is distinctly lacking in a physical component. I was glad of this, since I kept screaming into the void in front of me. I'm sure my throat would have been torn up long ago if it had been a physical action.

Finally, I felt somewhat purged of the anxiety, pain, confusion and fear that had become my constant state in the physical plane. I squawked one last time into the darkness of astral space and moved on. It had become so common for me to spend time in the astral plane each night, I barely noticed the oddities that once made me pay attention to my metaphysical surroundings.

I knew it wasn't right, how I had begun to treat the energetic and spiritual beings and entities with so little regard. That's how people ended up in trouble with tricksters and energy tainters. But it was my retreat from being so far out of my comfort zone, and I couldn't bring myself to be too concerned with consequences.

I moved alongside the Bifrost, vaguely curious about the silvery ribbon and what it meant to travel through it. I knew that if I could figure out how to really use it, I could go to any of the worlds and planes. I hadn't quite gotten to the point of taking the step to experiment with it, though.

Several of the worlds were pleasant, heavenly even. And that wasn't just a metaphor. They were the places our spiritual energies apparently went to after death. Based on the individual's actions and beliefs, they would be drawn to certain places, including the Summerlands, Valhalla, the Elysian Fields, and even Heaven or Hell.

I wondered about those places, but I wasn't sure I'd be able to accurately navigate between the worlds. The Summerlands would be great, but Muspelheim, the land of the fire giants, might be a bit too extreme for my enjoyment. So, I hesitated to explore the Bifrost more aggressively.

I reached out to touch the edges of the silver band, sensing the power of all the spirits traveling through it. I sighed, feeling a peace and satisfaction flow from the energies into my hand. It was the emotional energy of the dead at peace with their deaths. After a moment of indulgence, I pulled my hand back.

The world lurched violently, causing my eyes to cross and my stomach to roil. I fell to my knees and panted as the world righted and the adrenaline burst began to drain from my system. I let my head fall back, not sure who I was about to encounter this time, but annoyed either way. My gaze fell on a handsome man in a suit.

Only handsome wasn't the right word. The man was gorgeous in a way that only an immortal creature could be. Gorgeous in a way that drew in mortals, seduced them, made them prey to his predator.

I rolled my eyes and sighed. "Hiya, Lucy," I drawled. "How's tricks?"

Satan scowled at me. I was pretty sure I saw hints of a pout, as well.

"You know who I am," he said, his voice like melted chocolate flowing over my skin. "Yet you speak to me as though I am not dangerous."

I gave him a sardonic look. "No, Lucy. I speak to you as though you are just as dangerous no matter how I speak to you." I barked a laugh. "If you're gonna mess with me, at least I can control how I react to it. And if you're gonna kill me, at least I can get in a dig or two before I go down."

He watched me, considering my words. "So, it isn't that you don't respect my power..."

I shrugged. "More like, I can be helpless and scared shitless, or I can be helpless and snarky. And I love snarky."

Satan rubbed at his perfectly goateed chin. "Hmm."

I crossed my arms over my chest. "So?"

He cocked his head. "So?"

I rolled my eyes and threw up my hands. "So, what do you want? Why did you drag me here?"

He grinned a beautiful smile, showing perfect teeth. I almost shook my head when I noticed that they were so perfect there was even a tooth slightly askew, giving the grin a tiny flaw that made it even better.

"I was just wondering how my favorite antagonist was doing these days," he said with an intimacy in his voice that reminded me of our first meeting.

I shivered as the memory of his eroticism flickered through my mind. "I'm not *your* antagonist," I muttered. "I stopped Jehovah last time, remember?"

Satan's face twitched into an expression of lovely confusion for a brief moment. Then his smooth, sensual smile was back. I blinked, sure I'd seen wrong.

"Of course," he assured me. "That's why you're my favorite. You foiled all the plans my nemesis had made."

I kept my face smooth, but I was even more certain he was trying to cover up a slip.

But why would he have slipped in the first place? Unless he was on Jehovah's side last time. All of his actions fit that, but it didn't make any sense why he would deny that, or why he would be working with Jehovah to begin with.

"It was really quite the thing to watch," he continued. "I was impressed."

I scowled. "Glad to be of some entertainment to you, Lucy," I bit out. "I don't suppose you are going to take credit for the demons, at least? Aren't they your particular type of creatures?"

Satan shrugged. "The demons were a gift from Jehovah." He grinned. "That man – Bob – was far too fanatical in his religion to deal with..." he gestured at himself.

I snorted. "Demons are just fine, but a man in a suit? Oh no! Blasphemy!"

The epitome of evil threw his head back and roared with laughter. I grinned, unable to resist the infectiousness of his expression of joy.

The man quickly composed himself and looked me over carefully. "Really, now, Nicola," he drawled. "You haven't answered my query.

How are you doing?"

I frowned. There was a reason I hadn't responded to his earlier probe. If I were honest with myself, I'd have to admit that I wasn't sure how I was doing. Some days, I was just fine. But, lately, I'd just been feeling lost, like my life was careening out of control, specifically my control.

As for being honest with myself, I could feel myself flinch away from thinking about what was going on in my life. There were so many topics I was flinching from now. I needed to find something to give me stability, control. But the only thing I could seem to control these days was my travel into and out of the astral realms.

I hesitated as a thought crossed my mind. I wasn't entirely certain it would work but, if it did, it would be perfect. I crossed my arms and stared Satan down, waiting until his expression started to lose the edge of patience. Then I waved and stepped back into the physical realm.

Just before his face faded away, I saw it curl into an oddly familiar snarl.

• • •

I headed down the hallway towards the commons area for the after-supper show. Despite my fasting, I was expected to attend Zaro's display. I hobbled along slowly, still favoring my right foot. I wasn't really in the mood to smell the remains of the meal.

I turned the corner and nearly tripped over a young brunette girl, curled up on the floor in her cream linen dress, sobbing. I recognized her as the child who had called for her mommy weeks before.

I paused and then squatted down beside her, swaying awkwardly until I gave up and sat down with a thud. She looked up at me with red-rimmed eyes. She'd been crying a lot.

I gave her a tentative smile. "My name is Nicola. What's yours?"

"Maria," she whispered.

"Hello, Maria," I said, giving my words a formal slant. Kids liked being talked to like adults. "You seem to be having a rough day."

She hesitated and then nodded quickly. She ducked her head, staring at my bandaged foot.

I leaned forward to catch her eye. "As you can see," I said, lifting and wagging my foot at her. "I'm not doing so well either. You wanna talk about it?"

She bit her lip, glancing up at me several times before she nodded. "My mommy won't come back."

I frowned and leaned back. "Is it because she's busy with her new baby?"

Maria shrugged. "She said she wouldn't leave me after my brother was born, but then she did."

I nodded. "But your daddy takes care of you, doesn't he?"

She immediately shut down. Her face went blank and she stared into the space just above the floor tiles. I felt a tremor of anxiety coming from her.

"Is he your daddy?"

Her eyes flickered up to mine for a second. She stared at the tiles a moment longer before she shook her head quickly.

"Why does he take care of you, then? Is he your uncle?"

She shook her head again.

I reached out towards her, intending to pat her on the knee, but when she flinched, I drew my hand back.

"Do you want to stay with him?" I asked, nearly choking on the words, though I tried to keep my voice calm and even.

I watched tears drop off of her nose and she shook her head. "But, no one else wants me."

Her hoarse whisper nearly broke my heart. I pressed my lips together. "Then you can stay with me, Maria." I wasn't sure why I'd said it, but it felt more right than anything else that had happened in the last few weeks.

The girl looked up, and I caught the hope and fear in her eyes.

"I'll find out what needs to be done to make it official," I promised. "You won't have to live with that man anymore."

We stood up and I offered her my hand. She took it tentatively, before we continued walking to the commons area. We arrived just in time, finding two seats in the back just as Zaro took the stage.

For the first time since I'd arrived at the Center, I found myself ignoring the display of energy control, instead focusing on the lost little girl at my side. I felt incredibly clear and even clean, rather than muddled and muddied.

After the show, I took Maria's hand and we found Lupé. I settled Maria at a nearby table and took Lupé a few steps away. Lupé watched me with Maria with a look of curiosity and concern on her face.

"What's going on?" she asked.

I glanced at Maria. "I think her current situation is very healthy," I said. "I'd like to take her in myself."

Lupé frowned. "We don't usually approve of uprooting children once they are settled in with a caretaker."

"I get that." I folded my arms over my chest, ready to stand my ground. "What do I need to do to make this happen?"

Lupé stared at me for a long moment before relaxing her stance. "If that's what you want..." She waited for my firm nod. "Her mother will have to sign off on the new caretaker form," Lupé said.

I hesitated a moment, expecting more. "That's it?" I frowned. "So, the mother signed off on some random guy taking care of her kid?"

Lupé shrugged.

"I don't understand why the mother isn't taking care of Maria herself."

Lupé bit her lip.

"Look," I said, straightening my posture. "You seem really uncomfortable talking about this." I gestured towards the hallway where the rest of the center's Hands had departed. "No one else seems to be willing to answer my questions. What's going on with these mothers and their kids?"

"You are too... curious," Lupé said. She seemed to be searching for the right words. "Most people accept how we do things, but you demand to know why, how, everything. You dig so much."

"And that's a problem?"

"Well..." she hesitated. "Honestly, if I hadn't told Zaro you could see the energy, I doubt you would have been approved to go through the trials to join us."

I frowned. I felt rejected and insulted, but I couldn't put my finger on why I felt that way. "Oh. Well."

Lupé put her hand on my arm. "It's not that we don't like you, Nicola. You are just so... intense in your need to know. Most of the people here are much more laid back about such things."

I took a deep breath, surprised by how hurt I felt by her words. "I

71

see."

Lupé smiled at me. "I know you will be a great addition to our community. Especially once you experience Zaro's Peace."

I froze. Thoughts began clicking together in my mind. I worked to keep my expression neutral as I spoke. "Like you?"

The woman nodded, a faraway expression glazing over her eyes for a moment.

"Like Maria's mother?" I asked.

Lupé nodded again. "All of the Hands are blessed to have experienced the Peace. It's that experience, as well as the trials, that bind us together."

I nodded. "I think I understand." I paused a moment, considering how to proceed. "But I also need to understand why it is that the women in the Mother's Garden aren't the caretakers for their older children. Help me understand, Lupé."

Lupé looked down at the floor, then met my gaze. There was an urgency in her face and voice. "The mothers were blessed with those babies here at the Center. Those children are pure, untouched by the outside world. They must be cared for as such. The mothers can't focus as much on the blessed ones if they also have to care for the older ones."

I struggled to keep any reaction off my face. "And the men?"

Lupé shrugged. "It isn't perfect, but anyone who offers to become caretakers for the older children is welcomed. Many of us are too busy to take on the extra work of a child, and those with children already are discouraged from adding to their burden."

"I see," I said, not really understanding how a mother could throw away a child like that. A shot of guilt ran through me, and I pushed down the thoughts of my own little girl, so much like Maria. "Well, now that I understand how this works, I feel much better about the whole situation."

Lupé smiled, relief written on her features. "And Maria?"

I smiled back. "I'll have her stay with me tonight, and I'll talk to her mother tomorrow, first thing."

Lupé frowned but nodded. "Okay."

I talked Lupé into bringing an extra bed into my room for Maria, rather than trying to collect the one she'd been using from Roger. I told her it was too late to be bothering him, but I really didn't want to face down a possibly abusive man with only an unsure ally, at best.

Maria settled into her bed without a fuss, and I, for the first time in weeks, stayed out of the astral plane in case she needed me. The next morning, I took the girl to breakfast and watched her eat, trying not to drool over her food too openly. We went out into the garden as soon as she finished, caretaker forms in hand.

Once more, I was struck by the visual that the Mother's Garden presented. It was very obviously meant to separate the women and their babies from everyone else, giving them a certain status. I was a little surprised at the sudden feeling that I wasn't supposed to go into the space, but I glanced at Maria, squared my shoulders and walked through the gate.

Immediately, everyone stopped and stared at us. I stumbled a little, my balance still off without the missing toes. Insecurities pounded at me, draining my self-confidence. I ducked my head and nearly ran towards the woman I'd sought out.

"Excuse me," I began. "You are Eva? Maria's mom?"

The young woman frowned at me, then glanced down at the girl who looked just like her. "Her? Well, yeah."

I thrust the paper at her. "I would like to be her caretaker. Can you sign this?"

Eva frowned at the form but didn't move to take it. "What happened to Roger?"

I shrugged. "Maria isn't happy there. So I'm willing to take her." I waved the paper at the woman.

Eva stared at me a moment, then she shrugged and took the paper. "She'll be back with Roger when you have a pure baby, too, you know," she said, scrawling a signature.

I laughed nervously. "Oh, I won't be having children."

Eva raised an eyebrow and handed back the paper. "Why not?"

I frowned. "I'm not with anyone and not interested. Who would I get pregnant with?"

Eva smiled knowingly. "You'll see."

I felt a shudder go through me. "Besides, I'm..." I hesitated, unsure of how much to say. "I'm happy with my life as it is."

Eva laughed as she jiggled the baby on her lap. "That will change.

Trust me." The women around us nodded with identical, distant smiles on their faces.

I snatched the paper, grabbed Maria by the hand and dragged her from the garden. I felt bad about it, too, since the girl just stared back over her shoulder at the mother who didn't even speak to her.

"It'll be great, Maria," I said, trying to convince myself first. "We'll do just fine together."

CHAPT 12

I took a deep breath, gasping a little in the heavy humidity of the sauna. I was naked, except for a towel wrapped around my torso. I had noticed when wrapping the towel that I had lost enough weight to make my hip bones stick out a bit. My hair fell in thick black sweat-soaked strings around my face. I lifted a section of it away from my neck, vainly hoping it would bring some relief from the heat.

I glanced over at the man sitting just inside the door to the sauna. He was one of Zaro's loyal young protégés, and he was there to make sure that I didn't leave until I'd had an "appropriate" vision. Or passed out.

I took another labored breath in the hot wet air and tried to focus my concentration. I could enter a mindset that would allow for visions pretty easily, in most situations. That was one of the many skills I'd picked up over the years as an active participant in the Indianapolis Pagan community. I wasn't used to doing it in such strenuous conditions, however.

I'd been fasting since I'd left the fourth floor, so I hadn't even had the vegan diet that I'd been struggling with at the Center for the last several weeks. I felt weak and dizzy most of the time, and I often felt confused when people spoke to me. I'd been relying heavily on reading people's basic energies just to help me communicate with them, but I was still sure that there were a lot of non-sequiturs when I spoke to them.

In the last twenty-four hours, I'd just stopped talking to anyone other than Lupé and Maria, instead smiling and waving greetings rather than interacting with the brothers and sisters of the Center.

I felt myself dozing off and I shifted on the bench to wake myself up. If I didn't have the vision this time, I'd go back to fasting for another three days and then have to do this again. I wondered how many people faked a vision to try to pass this particular trial.

I adjusted my posture, straightening my spine and relaxing my limbs. I closed my eyes and struggled to picture a flame in my mind. This was one of the most basic meditation techniques, and I fed the flame with my frustration about how hard it was to hold the mental image of it.

I felt myself falling, like the feeling you sometimes get when you're falling asleep and it feels like you fell off of a curb or something. Only this wasn't a brief jolt passing through my body. It kept going. My empty stomach protested the way my body seemed to be flung around. I gritted my teeth and held on to the experience, hoping it was the beginnings of a real vision.

In my mind's eye, the darkness cleared back to reveal a cave. I smiled to myself. This was a good sign. I moved into the cave and carefully observed the hanging stalactites and their floor twins, stalagmites, lining the edges of a narrow path. There was no sign of life there.

I worked my way further into the cave, taking in the cool, moist air with a musty mineral smell to it. I listened to the rhythmic plink-plink of falling water drops. The dim interior was soothing rather than intimidating, and I felt a welcoming energy to the place.

The path ended in an arched opening with a warm orange glow shining through. I moved to the portal and peered into the next section. Dozens of candles burned on a flat stone pedestal in the center of the next cave. Each candle was made of white wax, and the drippings froze in their flow off of the chest-high table.

I smiled to myself. This was a pretty typical way for meditations and visions to begin. Maybe I could get some supper tonight. I stepped into the room.

Along the sides of the oval cave were treasures of all kinds: gems, jewels, necklaces, and crowns, paintings and sculptures, bejeweled swords, golden shields, and several large chests. I mentally counted the huge ornate boxes - five.

I moved to the nearest chest on my right, a fabric box with a lift-off lid made of tulle and lace over cream colored cotton. I opened it and pulled out a picture in a simple, but classy golden frame. In true vision fashion, I couldn't tell what the picture was of, though I knew it was something I was familiar with. I put the picture down and moved on to the next chest.

It was an opaque red crystalline box with gold hinges for the pyramid-shaped top. I hefted the chest open with a grunt at the surprising weight. I looked into the ruby chest and gasped. I pulled out the beautiful jade statue and looked at it closely.

The statue was done in a Buddha style, but the man it represented was not the typical Asian figure. In fact, it appeared to be a combination of two men, both of whom seemed strangely familiar to me. I looked at it until I was satisfied I would remember it, and I carefully placed the statue back into the chest.

The third box was a classic wooden pirate chest dripping with still-damp seaweed, and I turned the key to open it. Inside was a doll with dark hair and a flowered dress that looked familiar. I couldn't quite place what it meant, though, and I moved on after studying the doll enough to remember it later, as well.

The next chest was a flat square metal box with leather straps that had tribal designs burned into them, holding the box shut. I pulled at them to open it and peered inside. I pulled out a key with several symbols etched on it. I knew that I knew what the symbols were, though I couldn't see them clearly enough to recognize them now. I put the key in my pocket and moved on.

The final chest was a huge box of marble with a flat lid with an interior lip holding it in place. I shoved the lid aside and checked the contents. The box was filled with dust and grainy dirt. A child's skeleton was curled into a fetal position at the bottom of the marble chest.

I reached into the box and stroked the bare skull. My breath caught in my chest and I swallowed a sob. I felt heartbroken, angry and guilty over the skeleton, though I couldn't explain why. As I stared at the bones, I noticed a little bead bracelet around one of the wrists. I carefully lifted the arm up and removed the bracelet to take with me.

I immediately knew something was wrong. Maybe it was a shifting under my feet when I hadn't noticed the feel of the ground beneath me before. Maybe it was the way the candles seemed to dim. Maybe it was the way the lids to the chests all slammed shut. Or maybe it was the dark liquid that rushed in from the walls of the room, sloshing around the treasures without disturbing them and filling the space with several inches in a few seconds.

I turned to flee the cave and found the opening... gone. The arch was still there, but there was simply no hole in the wall where I'd come through. I pushed on the wall to check how solid it was. I knew I wasn't escaping that way. I turned back and sloshed through water that was already around my calves. I rushed around the room, scanning the irregular walls for anything to help me, but I found nothing.

I turned to the candles in the center of the room, examining the table and knocking candles off to see beneath them. I screamed with frustration when I couldn't find any clue as to how I could escape the black water, now up to my waist.

Despite having knocked all the candles off their stand and into the water, it wasn't too dark to see. I waded slowly through the water, unwilling to give up on escape. Taking a deep breath, I ducked down, looking under the water for something to use.

Soon the water was up to my neck, but I found a battle hammer made of gem-encrusted metal. I carried it to where the entrance had been and tried to swing it at the wall. My balance was completely off, though I managed to strike a glancing blow on the wall. Encouraged, I tried several more times.

Now the water was getting up to my eyes, and I had to let the heavy hammer fall so I could swim up to take a breath. I found my rhythm treading water, thankful I was a strong swimmer, and moved back over to the archway.

I hit the wall with my bare hands a few times out of frustration, but the memory of raging at the wall in my prison months before stopped me from going all out. Instead, I scanned the walls for a way out as the ceiling got closer and closer.

I took a few last deep breaths as the water reached the top of the cave and dove under. I had to find an exit or I would drown in this cave. I grabbed a sword and tried to pry at the wall until the blade slipped. The sword spun slowly away in the dark water, and I followed it with my eyes, helpless to do anything.

I gave up. I let my muscles go limp, just waiting until my body finally needed air enough to force me to inhale the liquid around me. I stared into the distance, realizing there was a light somehow. The light grew brighter, and I could see a shape coiling its way through the water towards me. My eyes widened when I saw that the creature had the long, sinuous tail of a sea serpent and the torso, arms and head of a woman.

The tail of the creature was glowing with a golden light from nowhere but reflecting off of the yellowish scales. The woman had skin of obsidian, with sparkling black diamond eyes. Her hair was a thick, tangled cloud of squid's ink flowing behind her. She smiled, flashing teeth of pearls, as she reached for me.

"I am here to help you," she said, though her mouth did not form words. "Why do you struggle alone?"

I gaped helplessly, and shook my head. She held me by the arms and pressed her lips to my forehead. The touch of her mouth was so cold, it burned my skin. She drew back, tight curls flowing around her head.

She spoke to me again in the smooth voice that didn't come from her throat. "Why don't you just breathe, now?" She nodded as though to reassure me, and it did. "Breathe. Now!"

•   •   •

I sat up and sucked in a lungful of air.

The sauna door was open, letting the cooler air in. Lupé, Nancy and Zaro were there, as well as the young man who had been guarding the door. I breathed deeply several times, glancing around and trying to get my bearings.

Zaro stood back and nodded at Lupé. She leaned forward, touching my arm to draw my attention. "Are you alright, Nicola?"

I nodded, still gasping a little. "I'm... fine. I was just ..." I took a deep breath. "I was drowning."

Lupé frowned.

"You were passed out," Nancy corrected me with her no-nonsense voice. "You must have fainted."

I shook my head. "No," I insisted, flinching away from her sharp look. "I was in a cave and there were candles and five chests, and I opened them all, and then the water filled up the cave, and I was drowning, until this beautiful fish-woman came and told me to breathe."

I looked up at Lupé and Zaro, avoiding Nancy's gaze.

Zaro frowned. "And you remember it all clearly?"

I nodded.

He turned to Lupé and shrugged.

Lupé nodded and smiled at me. "Wonderful!" she said. "You've had a vision."

I snorted. "Of course I did." I caught both Lupé and Zaro's surprised looks. "You do know I can open myself up to visions at will, right? I mean, it's not a hundred percent effective, but... " I shrugged.

Zaro must have realized he was standing with his mouth hanging open because he snapped his jaw shut, scowled and left the sauna. Nancy frowned at me but, finding nothing seriously wrong with me, followed him.

Lupé grinned. "I think you surprised him," she said.

I let the younger woman help me up, barely catching the towel before it slipped off of my body. "I'm not so sure that's a good thing," I muttered.

CHAPT 13

I stepped out onto the stage, squinting into the brightness of the spotlight. I swallowed around the lump in my throat and pressed my hand against the quivering in my belly. I hated being in front of people like this.

The feast I had eaten at lunch wasn't sitting so well with my stress. Since I'd passed my trials, my fasting was over, and the entire Center had celebrated my accomplishment. Every single one of the Hands had managed to shove a congratulations at me, despite my attempts to stay out of the spotlight.

I had just been glad to have some food in my stomach. Now, the vegan brownies that I'd eaten threatened to make a return. It had been so good to have food with a variety of flavors that I had overindulged. The Center food wasn't usually so well seasoned, and I'd been feeling the lack, especially during my three-day fast.

Embracing the sensual experiences of life was one of the ways I had always fed my spirit. I'd always been the kind to take that bite of cake or try the new dish at a restaurant. Not having that experience for so long had been weighing on me, leaving me feeling a loss of joy and hope.

Food was only one aspect of it, though. I'd also been feeling the lack of intellectual discussions, social interactions with those I'd bonded with over the years, and even the feeling of walking through the wild growth of the forests near my home. None of that was available to me here.

I stared out into the crowd, wondering how I was ever going to be able to make the Selection. I couldn't imagine turning so many people away, not when the Center was often their last hope for a longer life.

I peered out at the rows of people as Zaro bounded onto the stage, giving the introduction and welcome speech. I didn't hear a word of it. My eyes flicked from person to person as the man at my side explained the process.

Zaro nudged me, and I looked over at him. He was holding out a stylized scepter – the same one that I'd seen Nancy holding over the old man on the fourth floor. It had to be the Rod of Asclepius.

I blinked at him and reached out to take the Rod. It was about a foot long, made of a pearly white material. Intricate curly symbols were inlaid into the handle with a silver metal. There were three large silver pieces on the top, carved to look like serpent heads. Held between them was a large, perfectly clear crystal.

Zaro cleared his throat impatiently. I glanced up at him and took a deep breath as I turned back to the crowd. It was time to make the Selection.

I immediately skipped over the elderly, swallowing my guilt, but I knew I couldn't Select a grandmother at the expense of a child. Adults in their prime years were different. Many of them could be parents, and it broke my heart to not be able to determine that by the all-too-brief glances I gave them.

I was a creature of intellect. My default was to find the most logical answer. As hard as it would be, I would have been able to live with making a choice if I had all of the information. But I couldn't even do that. I had to guess at who the most valuable two people in the room were. And I had to do it without any data.

My eyes fell on a woman in the second row. Her brown hair was combed nicely, pulled back into a quick ponytail. She wore no make-up, and the beginnings of wrinkles showed on her face. Her clothes were clean and neat, but looked worn and old. She seemed resigned, glancing around at the crowd of hopefuls and pressing her lips together. Her eyes stayed low, as though she avoided looking at the stage. At me.

I held the Rod. I was the Hand that Selected. All of these people - I held their futures in my hands. I stared down at the children, gathered together at the front of the stage. A little baby in a blue jumper lay in his crib, eyes wide and staring at all the people, but not crying. A young girl with no hair smiled up at me. A boy in a wheelchair. A girl prone on a hospital bed. Children smiling. Children staring in awe. Children staring into space.

I blinked away the tears forming in my eyes. I glanced to the side at Zaro. He stood with his arms crossed, watching me without expression. I checked his energy and I could see the impatience building. I took a deep breath and looked back out into the crowd, this time looking for the energy clues that I hoped would guide my decision.

The smiling girl with no hair glowed with a green light, and I smiled back at her. She would be fine, with treatment. The baby also had a green glow about him, so I skipped over him, hoping they would be able to get what they needed elsewhere.

A flash of gold-orange caught my attention, and I looked over at a young man with a face so gaunt it was skeletal. His collar bones stuck out of his shirt and I could see the knobbiness of his shoulders through the fabric. The orange glow surrounded him, calling me to act.

I pointed the Rod at the young man. The audience applauded my first Selection, some politely, some enthusiastically. I felt slightly appalled by the clapping, and I rolled my shoulders to try to get rid of the feeling.

I scanned the crowd again, searching for another with the energetic indicators. I tried not to look at the faces of those I passed over. I found another gold-orange glow, and I pointed the Rod without pausing to see who it was. As the young woman lifted her hands to her mouth, crying with happiness at being Selected, I noticed another orange glow.

My eyes fell on the woman I'd noticed earlier. She looked even more dejected than before, but she smiled and comforted the two little girls who ran up to her, crying. I turned away, choking on the lump in my throat. The woman had no other options than what healing the Center could provide. And her children would lose her. Soon.

Tears filled my vision, and I stumbled towards the steps to leave the stage. A hand stopped me, and I stared into Zaro's face for a moment before releasing the Rod to his grasp. I ran off the platform and into the hallway through the door by the stage steps. I didn't stop until I'd reached my room, and I threw myself face down into the pillow before breaking into loud sobs.

My crying slowed down after several minutes, though the tears continued to run down my cheeks. I stared at the wall, not seeing the drywall and paint, but the brunette woman with her two children.

I heard the door open and close. Small footsteps approached. I rolled to my side and opened my arms to Maria. She allowed me to hold her until Kaitlyn came to take her to supper, though I refused to go. Instead, I fled into the astral plane.

• • •

I wandered around for a few moments before I realized where I wanted to go. I tried not to think about whether I could get there by myself, or if I was welcome to show up unannounced.

I closed my eyes and brought up the memory of the peaceful garden, the calm waters, the aromatic flowers. I immersed myself in the sensory memory and filled myself with energy, focusing it in the area of my diaphragm. The huge muscle clenched and I pushed the energy out to allow my will to be made real.

I felt a slight tilt of the world and a flash of silver-blue light. It was much like the feeling I'd had when I'd been brought to the garden, but not as rough or discordant, and the light was new. I kept my eyes closed a moment longer, hoping my attempt had worked. Finally, I peeked.

I sighed with relief and satisfaction. The slate and gravel walkway stretched out in front of me, passing in front of the clusters of bright flowers and grasses. I trudged towards the nearest bench and dropped down on the padded seat. I gripped the edge of the seat as a wave of guilt and memory washed over me. Once the worst of the wave passed, I lay back on the bench, throwing my legs over the end.

I stared up at the sky, noting in the back of my mind the oddity of the light - the garden was lit up as though it was dusk, but I was staring up into the blackest sky filled with millions of stars of all sizes and colors.

My eyes searched for the familiar patterns that I often saw in the patch of sky I could see between the tree branches while sitting on my patio at home. But Orion didn't hunt this sky, and the Northern Swan didn't fly among these stars.

I sighed and kept staring until the pinpoints of light blurred and I no longer saw the sky with my eyes. Instead, I saw the faces of the crowd. I could see the shocked baby boy, the old woman with the hunchback and a huge smile, the grinning girl with no hair, the confused old man with clouded eyes... the woman, holding out her arms to two young girls who cried so hard when she wasn't Selected.

I felt something touch the corner of my eye and I sat up quickly, surprised. I blinked the tears away from my eyes and stared at the old bearded man.

"You came to visit me," he said absently. "You have figured out who I am?"

I nodded and whispered, "Jehovah."

He nodded without looking at me. He was staring down at his hand, rubbing something between his fingers. I glanced down and saw a golden brown stone between his thumb and forefinger. I frowned at it, feeling like there was some kind of important meaning there, but the thought floated away like mist.

I struggled for a moment longer, trying to figure it out. Then I sighed.

I was always fighting myself these days, trying to go when I had no energy, trying to analyze when I had no information, trying to outmaneuver people without knowing their strategies. I looked up at the one called God and I remembered a quote that one of my high school friends had always said. "Let go and let God."

The quote had always bugged me. It struck me as really bad grammar. But there was something to say about letting the powers of our universe make themselves heard.

Well, they pretty much always tried to make themselves heard. I'd never met anyone with an ear for the gods and spirits say that it was too quiet. The spirit world liked being heard, and it was a rare enough occurrence that letting them know you would listen was like putting up a billboard offering free money with your phone number.

Generally, those who found that they were pretty good at communicating with gods and spirits also found that it was really important to figure out how to shut it off. Sleep and work were all too often necessities, while mouth-piecing for the gods was more of a side-job in modern times.

And it wasn't just about beings talking, either. The other aspect of listening to the powers was by way of omens and divination, such as palm reading, tarot cards, and even staring at clouds in the sky, which is legit for omens but hard as hell to interpret.

Like most people who walked a Pagan path, I'd learned tarot cards and a few other types of divination. I had a favorite deck of cards, as well as a handful of oracle decks, runes, and such. And I'd learned that the cards and other tools just help you hear what the powers are telling you.

The gods, spirits, and energies are always telling us all kinds of things about ourselves, about our world, about the people we interact with and the decisions we make. But we tune it out because it is so much information.

I don't need to read energies to tell me that my double caramel mocha latte is both hot and delicious. I just need the barista to hand that extra extra grande goodie over. I also don't need to know that the barista is having a stressful day. As a generally polite and patient customer, there's not much more I would be able to do for her. So to keep things less complicated, I don't read energies while ordering my coffee.

I could keep my energy sight on while driving, but then I'd see things moving around the edges of my vision. Not a great thing when you're driving down the road, or doing other things that require attention to the physical world.

In general, those of us who do these things learn to keep them shut off until we need them. We can't do everything always, and ignorance is bliss, or at least it lets you get a decent night's sleep.

Once a person got enough practice and experience reading energies, whether through a divination tool or not, they could put themselves into a mindset of allowing the powers to speak to them directly. Sometimes it was a god or spirit, and sometimes it was visions or intuition. Either way, it was a passive and receptive thing to do, not at all like the grasping and reaching I'd been doing.

I straightened my spine and let the mental spot just behind and below my ears open up. I suppressed a wistful smile when I realized how long it had been since I'd consciously thought about my personal method of listening.

A lot of people used their third eye or the spot at the top of their head to focus on opening their spiritual senses. Many, myself included, used different body parts depending on the situation. Most of the time, I used the little dent where my jaw attached to my skull.

I watched Jehovah's face as my perception of everything changed.

One of the reasons I didn't often use my energy sight, other than for brief glimpses, is that it can be distracting, confusing and surreal. Everything ends up with an energy form superimposed over it. The energy form looks like a semi-transparent blob of color, like when you stare at a picture for several seconds and then look at a white space to see the inverse image. This after-image shows color and shape, which combine to give the seer clues to the person or item.

Not everyone sees images as clearly as others, though. And I had met witches that heard sounds, or smelled scents. One had even felt textures. Most had a combination of these not-quite-there sensory inputs, which told them what they needed to know – if they could figure out what the symbology meant.

And books were little help on that. A list of color meanings could give you an idea of what green meant, but a yellow-green and a rich forest green could mean opposite things. A person who hates the color yellow will see it in negative situations, while a person who loves yellow will interpret it as a positive energy. The seer's mood can also affect the way their perceptions present themselves.

I always felt that what a person perceives when they open themselves up is not necessarily what is being shown. It is how each person's brain interprets the information of energy. The information is coming in from a source that is not treated as being as real as the physical world. It is coming in through senses that have no words or context. Our parents teach us colors and textures, but they don't teach us how to perceive the energy of solemnity or how to translate the way a moss-covered boulder communicates.

We have to not only learn to open ourselves up to the information, but then we have to process that information through brains that only understand certain sensations, like sight and smell and emotions. Those are the filters that the powers of the universe speak through. And we have to figure out what the hieroglyphs mean.

I watched Jehovah's mouth move, but I was too focused on opening my senses to catch what he said. His eyes flicked up to my face in almost slow motion. I stared in fascination as the colors swirled and took shape, changing how his face appeared, showing me another face on top of his.

Jehovah, the face behind the colors, stared a moment before his eyes widened, eyebrows raising high. Then his eyebrows dropped, and his face contorted into a scowl. But I'd already seen it. My eyes narrowed as I watched Jehovah's features become nearly masked by the face of Satan. I wasn't sure what it meant, exactly, but it was an important revelation.

I pressed my lips together and glared at the god for a moment before I stepped back, escaping into the physical world.

CHAPT 14

Lupé knocked and opened the door. It was late, and Maria was already snoring lightly on her own bed. I watched Lupé enter with no desire to welcome her, but I also didn't tell her to leave. I moved my legs for her and sat up. She sat down on the corner of my bed and took a deep breath.

She watched me for a few minutes. I ignored her, staring at the wall above Maria's bed. Finally, she shifted, and I knew she was going to tell me why she had come.

"It gets to everyone," she said. "The first time we Hold the Rod and make the Selection."

I thought about the woman and her children and held my tongue.

"I've always thought that we should prepare the Hand somehow," Lupé continued. "But I couldn't figure out any way to do it. No matter how long I thought about it, there was just no way to let someone understand the pain and guilt."

I snorted. "We could pick more than two," I mumbled.

Lupé patted my leg. "That would be the best way," she admitted. "But Nancy has shown us that it's not possible. The Rod is too weak to do more than two. It's best to just accept that and know that we do what we can."

She threw a glance at me. "It may be your nature to understand," she said, "but it will tear you up if you don't believe that what we do is really for the best."

Embracing that kind of dogmatic belief was how people defended against doubts of their own actions. It was much the same reasoning that led people to doubt someone could commit a crime because "he was such a nice guy" or "she was so friendly". It kept people from having to admit they might have been dreadfully, terribly wrong.

And it was so tempting to me. To accept that the Center had been doing this for so long, to believe that all options had been explored and that my choices had not been about denying so many, but that they had been a matter of giving a gift to a fortunate few. It would be a relief to know that the problem wasn't that I, personally, denied the gift of Healing to people, but that the Rod was inadequate for the task of Healing so many.

The Rod that I had pointed into the crowd was the problem. Not me. Not my choices. The Rod was the weak spot because Nancy could only use it on so many people within a certain period of time.

My mind relaxed at the thought, replacing the sick woman with an image of Nancy Healing the two Selected. Only it wasn't the Selected she was Healing. It was an old man with money.

I frowned. "The Rod is what is used to heal," I said, slowly. "Like actually used, as a tool?"

Lupé nodded, and I caught the movement out of the corner of my eye. "That's what Nancy says. That's why she has access to the Rod at any time."

I cursed myself for being so stupid. I had been holding it in my hand and I never thought to check it for a Runespell.

"Nancy uses the Rod to heal the Selected," Lupé said, trying to comfort me with her words. "She will use it over the course of the week to heal the Selected that you chose. You saved those two people."

I paused. "Nancy is going to Heal the Selected this week. Up on the fourth floor?"

"Yes." Lupé was watching me closely now, but I ignored her. Pieces of the puzzle had started clicking into place inside my head for the first time in weeks.

Nancy had the Rod of Asclepius. Based on what I'd seen on the fourth floor that night, and despite what Lupé and the rest of the Hands believed, she was using it on more than just the Selected. For money.

I nearly gagged on that thought. The Selected weren't just the poor ones who wouldn't be able to afford whatever Nancy was demanding in payment. People were dying because of the two-person rule she had apparently created. To create a false demand.

The woman and her two children flashed through my mind again.

I choked on the memory. At least that explained why the Center didn't need to rely on massive donations from its members or those they Healed through the public rituals. Figures I'd get thrown in with such a bass-ackwards type of cult.

I shook my head as if clearing it. I shot Lupé a wry smile, trying to pick up the thread of conversation again. "I guess it wouldn't be kosher to watch the Healing, huh?"

Lupé shook her head. "Healing is a private matter," she confirmed. "But the Healed often come to thank the Hand that Selected them, afterwards."

I nodded, staring into space. I needed to find the sigil, but I was only mostly certain it was in the Rod. I wouldn't have many chances to get the Runespell, so I needed to know for sure. Ideas formed in my rusty mind, and I latched onto them, desperate to lose myself in my intellectual comfort zone and use my logic to find the answers.

Lupé said something and I nodded absently. She stood and left the room, but I only barely noticed that she was gone.

A few moments later, the thought hit me. I went to the small dresser and pulled out my digital recorder. I had been lax in making notes each night, but I still managed to record my observations some of the time.

I paused before I tapped the record button, gathering my thoughts. I quickly outlined my experience as the Hand, trying not to dwell on the emotional burden. When I finished and returned the recorder, I sat down on my bed, crossing my legs in front of me. I took several deep breaths, closing my eyes and focusing on the air moving in and out of my lungs.

I sent my mind back to earlier in the day. I remembered stepping out onto the stage, feeling the heat of the lights, the shifting sounds of the crowd in front of me. I smelled my own sweat and the subtle sweet stench of sickness.

I felt the weight of the Rod in my hand. I remembered the pearled handle and the silver engraving going up the shaft. I pulled on the details of my memories, searching them. I combed over the memory of the three serpent-head prongs and the crystal held by them.

I reviewed the memories over and over, drawing more and more details from them, searching for anything that might be the sigil I was looking for. I was close to giving up when I found it.

The pyramid shape of the curved-trillion cut crystal was held in place by the serpent's heads on three sides of it around the top portion. But the point on the bottom rested on something else: a silver shape inlaid into the top of the pearled cylinder that formed the shaft handle of the Rod. And though it did not match any of the four sigils that I wore on the chain at my throat, it was similar enough.

I took a deep breath and opened my eyes, breaking out of the mild trance that I used to revisit my memories. I smiled wryly to myself. I'd found the healing sigil, but how was I going to retrieve it?

● ● ●

My discovery had two major effects on my behavior, and people noticed.

First, I stopped asking questions about Zaro and Nancy and the Selection and the Healing. Lupé seemed to think that my experience and her answers to my questions had simply managed to satisfy my curiosity. Most of the brothers and sisters of the center appeared to believe that my turn as the Hand that Held the Rod had made me a true believer in their cause. The temptation of that belief still pulled at me, trying to alleviate the periodic bouts of guilt I felt.

Kaitlyn, with a surprising bitterness in her voice, asked me if I'd found what I was looking for.

I paused, wondering if she suspected that I was really there to steal the Healing sigil. Then I realized the incredible coincidences that would have to occur for that to happen. I reconsidered her question. She must have thought I was there to find some kind of inner peace, like the others.

I shrugged. "I doubt anyone here would even be able to completely understand what it is that I'm looking for," I said.

Kaitlyn frowned. "What do you mean by that? What are you looking for?"

I grinned and leaned forward. Kaitlyn leaned towards me, expecting a secret. "I'm looking for a magic pendant that was created by the Norse god, Odin. And I'm pretty sure Nancy keeps it in her pocket."

The woman pulled back. She scowled at me. "That's not funny."

I looked her right in the eye and smirked at the irony. "I'm not joking."

She walked away, but she looked back at me several times.

I shook my head. Her suspicions had made her a liability, though I hoped our friendship wouldn't be too damaged by how I'd handled it. I would need her help before all of this was over. At least, that's what I interpreted from my vision in the sauna. I'd become convinced that the dark woman in my vision was Yemaya, an African healing and water goddess. I also felt that Yemaya came to me to let me know that Kaitlyn was going to be an ally.

The second way my behavior changed was that I had focus for the first time since I'd arrived at the Center. I wasn't floundering around. I wasn't unsure of if I should even be there. I wasn't confused by everything around me.

I knew what I was looking for and, perhaps more importantly, I wasn't afraid to use my energy sight to cut through the secrecy and illusions that kept the visitors and new members off-balance.

An unforeseen side effect of using energy work so much was that I didn't feel as weak from the diet. I still felt like my skin was getting too tight, like I was shrinking in on myself. My teeth still felt achy and loose. My stomach occasionally pounded at my ribs, as if begging for the kinds of foods I found satisfying. I still felt light-headed more often than I liked, and the thought of bacon made my mouth water more than I liked.

But I didn't feel as muddled. It was as though I was still low on energy, but the efficiency of my energy use went up.

Unfortunately, I also learned more about how people felt about and were treated at the center. Within a few days, I notice Lupé's energy was rapidly changing through several negative emotions, including anger and fear. I had promised Ames I would look after her. And I would keep that promise.

CHAPT 15

I searched Lupé out on one of the meditation benches while I was walking through the gardens. She seemed to be deep in thought, and her energy was all over the place again. Her lips were pressed together and she was frowning at the ground in front of her feet.

Maria had gone off to play with some of the other children her own age, and I found I didn't need to watch her closely during this time of the day. This freed me to explore the grounds and talk to people while technically being occupied with childcare, which kept me off of garden and household chores duty.

"Can I join you?" I asked, pitching my voice low so I wouldn't startle the younger woman.

She glanced up at me and stared a moment before she scooted to one side to make room.

I sat down and took a minute to admire the beauty of the desert plants. A Joshua tree stood nearby, looking alien and giant. A huge blue agave squatted next to the bench, nearly five feet tall with large aloe-like leaves clustered in a half-circle. A similar-looking yucca sat on the other side of us, with flat sword-shaped leaves and a tall cluster of white flowers that towered nearly seven feet in the air. Bright yellow flowering Chamisa bushes with lacy leaves edged along the back of the bench. A patch of bold red coralroot grew directly across the path from our seat.

I took a deep breath, enjoying the cool breeze that cut the sun's heat just enough. Then I turned to the younger woman.

"What's the matter, Lupé?"

She shook her head.

I reached over and took her hand. "Tell me," I pleaded. "I won't tell anyone else. Trust me. Please."

She looked up, meeting my eyes. She gave me a long, searching look. I could tell she was hoping she could trust me. I let her take as long as she needed. I didn't want to spook her.

"I shouldn't feel like this," she began.

I squeezed her hand gently.

"It's an honor," she said, quietly. I had to lean forward to catch her words as she continued. "I just... I don't want it. I should, but I don't."

I held her hand for a long moment, but she didn't clarify.

"What is it, Lupé?" I asked, keeping my voice as quiet as hers. "What honor are you talking about?"

The young woman shrugged her shoulders and started to turn away.

"Is it about the Rod?" I asked, grasping at any idea.

"No," she said. "Nothing like that."

I pulled her hand towards me, gently, opening myself up to the energies I was about to use. "Lupé, you've always been so open and honest with me. I don't know if I could have handled being kept in the dark about so many things." I paused. "You told me stuff I needed to know, even when you maybe shouldn't have."

I waited for her to nod. I fed a tiny thread of hope into her through our joined hands.

"Please," I said. "Don't keep this from me. Don't throw me back into the dark with all of the secrets and hush-hush stuff. Let me know what is going on. Even if I can't help. Even if it changes nothing, you won't be carrying the secret alone."

Lupé frowned, but she didn't direct it at me. She seemed to be thinking, and I hoped my plea had gotten to her. I added a hint of the feeling that comes from sharing things with friends and pushed that small bit of energy through my hand to hers.

"I've gotten a proposal," she said.

It was so odd a thing, so different from anything I could have expected. It took me a moment to understand what she'd said. "Oh," I stammered. "Like, marriage?"

She nodded.

"Um, okay." I turned over her statement in my mind. "Who proposed to you?"

Lupé shrugged her shoulders. "Zaro, of course."

I nodded. "Of course." Then I frowned. "Isn't he already married? To Nancy?" I shivered at the thought of the emotionless nurse.

The younger woman nodded. "Zaro is married to Nancy, first. But he has taken many other wives, as well." She glanced over her shoulder.

My eyes followed her gaze behind us. The Mother's Garden.

"Wait a minute," I said, as pieces started clicking into place. "Is Zaro married to all the women who go to the Mother's Garden?"

Lupé nodded.

"And the blessed babies?" I asked in a whisper. "All of them are his children?"

She nodded again.

"Is that why they are blessed?"

Lupé's eyes darted to mine, and I pushed down a jolt of fear that I'd overstepped with my questions. "I... I don't know," she said. "I never thought about it... like that." She paused. "I guess that could be."

I took Lupé's other hand, holding both of hers in both of mine. I waited until she looked me in the eye and I held her gaze. "Lupé," I said in a measured tone. "Do you want to marry Zaro?"

"No," she whispered. She shook her head and pulled her hands away. "It's an honor to be asked," she said. "I shouldn't refuse."

I nodded. "When?"

She looked up. "Tomorrow night."

"Is there a public ceremony for his marriages?"

She shook her head. "Most don't even know there was a marriage until the woman tells them. And that usually happens when she is blessed with a child."

I nodded my understanding. "You can say no."

Lupé shook her head. "If I say no, Zaro will withdraw the blessing of Peace," she explained. "I would never be able to feel the touch of pure contentment again."

I frowned. "Is it that great?" I asked. "I mean, really that great?"

Lupé nodded. Her eye unfocused as she remembered. "It really is."

I nodded, accepting what she'd said but not really understanding it. "Okay."

We sat in silence for a moment. I stroked Lupé's hand in a soothing gesture, thinking over her problem the whole time.

"I think I know a way to help," I said, breaking the silence.

She looked up, startled, and I patted her hand and smiled at her.

"Just let me try," I said. "He'll never know it came from you. I promise."

She frowned but nodded.

CHAPT 16

I sat down on my bed, holding the recorder. I'd just finished making an entry, and I was turning my plan over in my mind. Kaitlyn had agreed to watch Maria for a few hours, and I was going to meet with Zaro before the evening meal.

I thought again about Lupé's reaction to the idea of losing Zaro's Peace. It was like her entire mind and spirit was drawn to it. I'd never seen anything like it, on an energy level.

Except I had. Every single night, I'd watched people craving the Peace. Even I had craved it more often than not, and I'd never actually experienced it.

"Our favorite thinker."

"Deep in thought."

I jerked upright and swung my eyes to the side at the sound of the familiar voices. My mouth cracked into a huge grin when I caught sight of the twins.

"Huginn! Muninn! Where have you been?" I gushed.

The human-looking creatures exchanged hooded glances.

"We've been here," said Muninn.

Huginn nodded. "Waiting near."

I frowned. "You mean, here at the Center?"

The two nodded.

"Why haven't I seen you? Why didn't you come and talk to me?"

Muninn's hair moved like ruffling feathers. "Your eyes see us only when your mind sees us."

Huginn cocked his head to one side. "Your eyes don't see when your mind is blind."

I bit my bottom lip, considering that. "So, I haven't been able to see you because my mind has been so clouded and confused?"

The twins bobbed their heads in unison.

"Well," I said. "I'm doing better now."

I glanced at the small alarm clock on top of the dresser, and I jumped up off the bed. "Unfortunately, your timing sucks," I said. "I have a meeting that I can't miss."

The twins exchanged glances again. I cut them off before they could say anything, though.

"Come back around the same time tomorrow," I said, trying to be reassuring. "I'll have time alone and we can talk."

I dropped the recorder in the dresser drawer and grabbed the ravens in a hug before I turned and rushed out the door. I frowned when, halfway down the hallway, I realized how sad and anxious they'd looked when I left them. I decided I would ask them about it the next day.

I rapped my knuckles against the door to Zaro's room. He opened it and waved me inside.

Like my own room, it was a single room with only a bed and a dresser for furniture. However, the bed was a large king-sized bed with huge fluffy pillows and blankets that looked soft and comfortable. The dresser was also bigger with a mirror on top and a collection of fancy boxes and jewelry scattered among bottles of cologne and several incense burners.

"What can I do for you, Nicola?" Zaro asked in his smooth tenor voice.

I turned to look at him, taking note of his appearance for the first time in a long time. I'd always just noticed the overall impression of him: smooth, polished, rather typical for a self-help guru type. Up close, he seemed surprisingly... average.

He had very dark brown hair, cut short enough that it barely stayed in the parted style he kept it in. His skin was warm cream color, with just enough golden undertones to indicate he would tan easily in the sun.

He had dark brown eyes that veered into nearly black. They were well spaced in his face, which was clean and free of any blemishes. He had a nice jawline, and his chin was a little too weak to bring the rest of his features together to make a handsome man. Instead, he was just... okay looking.

He smiled at me, obviously trying to put me at ease and urge me to talk. His teeth were even and white, but not too much so. He even had a slight dimple on one side that, if slightly more prominent, would have taken his face from regular to handsome.

I straightened my shoulders, determined to do what I'd set out to do. "I'm here to talk to you about Lupé," I said.

His eyes widened slightly. He hadn't expected that to be what I'd asked him to talk about.

I pushed on before he could interrupt. "I know you asked her to marry you," I said. "But you need to withdraw your proposal. She is too young, and the situation here," I gestured around, indicating the Center, "well, it's pressuring her to accept. And that's not right. You shouldn't be using your position to push young women, barely of age, into marrying you."

I paused, taking a breath. I wasn't really sure where to go from there, so I waited for Zaro's reaction. He watched me carefully as I spoke, with curiosity but not concern. When I stopped, he stepped forward, coming too close. He was only a few inches taller than me, but his posture felt intimidating.

"This situation," he began, "is none of your concern." He held up a hand when I opened my mouth to reply. "Lupé may be someone you care about, but this is her choice – to accept or refuse the honor of my marriage bed."

I blinked. "Bed?" My eyes narrowed as the suspicions I'd brushed away came back. "Is this about sex?"

Zaro grinned. "That is none of your concern either, unless..." He trailed off, stepping back as his eyes tracked down the length of my body.

I'd been to clothing optional events, walking completely nude in a crowd of people. I'd felt less naked then than I did under his scrutiny.

"What you are doing is wrong," I said, taking a step back and trying not to move my hands to cover my body. "You can't treat people this way."

Zaro's face hardened. "No one has ever complained," he said. "And you won't find anyone who ever will. There are no victims of mine among the Hands that Hold the Rod."

I shivered at the innuendo he put into the words. I pulled myself together and tried again.

"You will leave Lupé alone," I said, shocked at how much my voice was shaking. I couldn't believe how terrified I was about standing up to this man. It made no sense that a mere guy should be so powerful a figure to me, who faced down gods and demons. I wasn't the bravest person ever, but I was braver, and better, than that.

He stepped forward, a gleam in his eye that frightened me more than I ever thought I could be frightened by a mortal man.

"Then I'll have you, instead," Zaro said. "And Lupé will still be mine. Later, but she will be mine."

The casual way he spoke the words wasn't a threat. There was no malice and no doubt. Icy fingers clawed at the back of my head. The fear clouded my mind and clotted in my gut, forming a ball of cold terror.

I gasped as I realized I'd lost control of the conversation. Panic set in. Before I could do something to make the situation worse, I turned on my heel to leave. If I was completely honest, I was desperate to retreat.

Zaro calmly reached out and ran his hand up my arm. Instantly, I felt a warmth rush through my body, like a blanket on a cold, winter day. My eyes went unfocused and my limbs fell limp.

I could feel Zaro's hands on my body, groping at my breasts and sliding along my belly. His mouth fell on my shoulder, and he pressed his lips along my collarbone. It didn't matter. I'd never felt such peace. It enveloped me, shoving out any discomfort. Even the knowledge that the man was using my body wasn't enough to break through the layers of contentment that swathed my mind.

I felt his hands under my blouse, taking it off as his mouth made wet tracks over my chest and down towards my nipples. The satisfaction of warm cocoa slid over my tongue, drowning out the protest that had started forming in my mind.

I heard him murmur between my breasts, "Congratulations on your wedding, Nicola. Now you are mine, and your children will be mine."

The warmth of a hot bubble bath pushed away the image forming in my head, the image of a little girl hugging me tightly. The little girl dissolved and I sighed with contentment. The softness of warm fluffy clouds muted the feeling of Zaro taking off my bra and pants. The fuzziness of waking up to the sound of birds and laughing children covered up the feeling of his hands at my crotch.

A sudden shock jolted me out of my muddled mind. I blinked up at the ceiling for a moment before I realized that the shock was from Zaro driving home as he consummated my unwanted marriage. My knees were pressed against my chest, giving him easy access. I gargled a protest, trying to push my legs down and struggling to sit up.

Zaro paused in his thrusting, laying his body across mine and pinning me down. He reached for his neck and grasped the wire pendant with his right hand while stroking my face with his left. I felt his pelvis jerk against mine twice before my eyes rolled back with the taste of rich tiramisu gliding down my throat.

I barely noticed the bed jerking rhythmically underneath me as I relaxed into the mattress and indulged in the feelings Zaro fed my mind while he raped my body.

• • •

I lay on my narrow, lumpy bed, staring at the ceiling all night. After what had happened, I couldn't sleep. I'd just walked through the evening in a daze, barely noticing what Maria had said at supper or when I put her to bed.

I wasn't afraid, though a part of me felt that I should have been. I also thought I should have been angry, but there was nothing like that either. In fact, the only emotion I could identify was longing.

I was longing for the peace and comfort that I'd felt under Zaro's Touch. Even as I tried to process everything else about the experience, there was no connection, no reaction. It was unsettling to me, but I didn't really feel unsettled.

I was the type to get angry for a victim I'd read about in a news article. I had to be careful about reading certain books because my empathy for the characters would actually change my behavior. I could even feel a wide range of emotional reactions for the other women that Zaro had forcibly "married." But I felt nothing about my own experience.

Except for the urge to go back to him and beg him for another

Touch. I smiled at the memory of how wonderful it felt, how at peace I was. It wasn't a strong feeling, like joy or excitement. Even happy was almost too active a feeling for what I'd experienced. I had been content, for the first time in a long time. Possibly for the first time in my life. And I just wanted to sink into that feeling again.

I frowned as I realized the turn my thoughts had taken.

What Zaro had done to me was wrong on so many levels. I should feel angry, scared, hurt, betrayed, violated, sad... anything. But the memory of the blue-white cloud of Zaro's Touch misted over thoughts of what I should feel.

I latched on to the last bit of will I could find in my heart and embraced my recent addiction. I fled into the astral plane.

• • •

I walked around in a daze, mechanically going through the motions. I woke up Maria in the mornings, and we dressed before breakfast. We attended workshops and classes as dictated by Zaro's schedule for the Center, then ate lunch before heading out to the gardens.

Now that Maria was settled in, I picked up a few gardening shifts, so I pulled weeds and picked produce while Maria played with her friends in the sunshine. We ended the day with the evening meal and Zaro's display.

Each day, he chose another girl, usually between twelve and twenty-five years old, and he gave her the Touch of Peace. Each day, I joined all the other women who had previously experienced that touch in staring longingly at the lucky girl.

If Zaro had indicated in any way that begging would get us another taste of that comforting feeling, I would have pushed my way to the front of the stage to fall on my hands and knees at his feet. Instead, I took Maria back to our room and put her to bed, distracted by the thoughts of how to earn Zaro's Touch and the memories of it.

Once Maria was settled in her bed, I lay down and tried not to cry from my sorrow and longing. Each night, I choked on the tears just beneath the surface until I finally fled into the astral plane.

My experiences of the astral plane had not gone unaffected, either. The landscape these days was muted colors and sparse plant life. Even the creatures of the astral plane seemed to steer clear of me, except for a growing collection of shades, specters, whispers and fades, all creatures that feed on sorrow and despair. Those small scavengers followed me around wherever I went, though I seldom bothered to notice them.

Twice in my astral excursions, I felt the world start to tilt around me. I didn't care to deal with the games of Jehovah/Satan, or whatever else he wanted to convince me he was. I simply stepped back into the physical realm when I felt the pull.

The routine of life at the Center became my stability while I waited to be summoned by Zaro. And he did summon me.

Twice I hurried to his room when he sent me the message. Twice I rushed to obey him when he told me to take off my clothes before he would touch me. Twice I ignored the disgust and filth I felt at his use of my body while my mind swam in seas of pleasant sensations.

And twice I spent the rest of the night staring at the ceiling, confused and lost.

CHAPT 17

Kaitlyn put her hand on mine when I started to stand up from my seat at the breakfast table.

"Nicola, can I speak to you for a moment?"

I dropped back down into my seat. I picked at the scraps of oatmeal on my bowl until the room was emptied.

Kaitlyn took the bowl to put it in the dirty dish bin. She hesitated and caught my eye, nodding at Maria sitting on the bench behind me.

I turned in my seat to look at her. She seemed unhappy, curled up into herself. She looked too much like she had when I first met her. I stared at the young girl with her head hanging down and her hair covering her face from view.

"What's wrong, sweetie?" I asked, reaching towards her, putting as much emotion into my voice as I could manage.

She flinched away from my touch and I pulled back, confused by her actions. What had I done that made her react that way to me? I glanced up at Kaitlyn. Her mouth was pressed together like she was trying really hard not to speak up. I turned my gaze back to Maria and waited.

She took a shaky breath. "I tried to talk to you," she said, so quietly I had to strain to hear her. "I tried, and you wouldn't answer me."

I leaned forward, heartbroken by her words. No child should feel ignored.

"I'm sorry about that, Maria," I said, trying to let her know how much I meant it by the tone of my voice. "I know I was really distracted. I admit that. But it won't happen again."

She shook her head. I drew back, not sure what she was trying to tell me. Before I could think of something to say, she looked up at me. Her eyes were filled with tears, and I gasped at how much sorrow filled her face.

"It will happen again," she whispered.

"Why do you think so?" I asked.

She shut her eyes tightly, tears squeezing out onto her cheeks. Her voice was so choked, I almost missed her words. "Because that's what happened with Mommy."

I recoiled from her words, biting back my denial.

Kaitlyn stepped in, holding Maria close. "What happened with your mommy?" She asked.

Maria looked up into the woman's compassionate black eyes. "Mommy went to Zaro," she explained. "Then she was married to Zaro. Every time she visited him, she ignored me."

Maria's mouth trembled as she tried to get the words out. "She said she was missing the best thing that ever happened to her." The girl sniffed. "She used to say that I was the best thing that ever happened to her. But she found something she loved more."

Maria looked at me. "Now you found it, too," she said. "And I'll be ignored again until a new baby comes. Then I'll go live with a man who..." She broke down in sobs. "Why doesn't Mommy love me anymore?"

I felt sick to my stomach at her words. How could a mother be so entranced by Zaro that she would forget her own daughter?

"Why don't you love me?"

I froze. It wasn't that I didn't love her. I was more like I no longer loved at all. But I wasn't like Maria's mother. She stopped loving her own child. I...

No.

No. I hadn't forgotten Ella. I mean, I hadn't really thought about her in... Sweet Baby Baldur, what date was it? How long had I been here? But Ella was fine. She was with my mother. It wasn't like I'd abandoned her. And certainly not like Maria's mother. Right?

But I had stopped moving forward. I had stopped thinking of going back home. I had stopped considering my life after the center. After Zaro's Peace.

No, the Peace was so good. It couldn't be a bad thing to feel so... loved and warm and comfortable. The things Zaro did while giving me Peace, though. That was on the bad side. What he did was...

It was a small price to pay for such a feeling. Letting him touch me wasn't really that bad. After all, I hadn't even fought him off.

I stood up, backing away from Maria and Kaitlyn... and the truth. I felt the heavy darkness of panic pressing against the edges of my vision, pushing on my skull like a physical thing. I gasped for breath, choking on the air in my throat.

The backs of my legs hit the bench behind me. I spun around, leaned over the bench and gagged, trying not to vomit.

Zaro had never asked. He used the power of his Peace to suppress my resistance. What he had done to me – to all the women here – was rape. And I forced myself to accept that. And I fought to accept that I had to force myself to accept such a thing.

I lay across the bench and choked on my sobs, trying to wrap my mind around the facts.

He had power. It took away my will to fight. I wanted it again. I wanted it so much, that I had accepted that he would rape me again. I wanted it so much, that I had emotionally abandoned my daughter and my life outside of the Center. I had abandoned Maria.

I knew this. It made sense. It fit. It was correct. But I still wanted it... Like a drug.

My head jerked upright.

Like a drug. I turned the thought over in my head. I'd seen people get addicted to draining energy from others. It gave them a bit of a high feeling. Generally, they stopped because it also made them more likely to lose control or get empathic sensations that could be less than pleasant to deal with.

Energy as a drug. It wasn't a new concept, but there was rarely a pusher. Or was Zaro a dealer? A street-corner pimp? I shook my head. That was way too appropriate an image. And way too raw on my nerves. That son of a bitch got us hooked on the Peace that he offered. And that was only the beginning of his crimes.

I tried to feel angrier about the whole thing, but I just felt like I'd been emotionally kicked in the gut. I felt sad, and weak, and confused, and needy.

But at least I no longer felt like Zaro was the solution.

• • •

I stayed in my room all day, thinking about my stay at the Center, about the things that I'd seen and the things that I'd suspected.

I thought about going into the astral plane, but the new idea that Zaro's touch of Peace was like a drug had me reconsidering. What if I was actually addicted to the astral plane, too?

I paced the small area between my bed and Maria's. What should I do? What were my options?

I found myself stopping and staring into space, longing for the comforting sensations of the Touch. Each time, I shook myself out of it, half-heartedly berating my own weakness.

I felt untethered, like there was nothing holding me to reality. I was just passing through the physical realm, a ghost, unaffected and unaffecting. Even my anger and disgust, after the first jolt of emotion, had faded to a pale hint of the feelings I knew I should be having. I tried to remember the last time I'd felt so lost and disconnected.

I stopped.

Keith.

I remembered.

I plopped down in the cracked maroon vinyl seat of the booth and rasped out a request for coffee and water to the server. I dropped my head on my arms. Keith was dead. A few days before, we had been watching him with suspicion, trying to figure out his game. And now he was dead. He'd entered into a devil's bargain for Ella, our daughter.

I'd felt so removed from everything. Even my senses had been dulled while I was working through the shock of my former lover's death. I remembered the feeling of... not feeling.

It wasn't just emotional. My ears had felt full and I'd had difficulty seeing clearly. Even the nerves in my skin seemed to stop picking up signals for temperature and pressure. Walking across a floor felt odd, with no sensation of the ground under my feet. Even emotion-filled memories were nothing more than recalling details. The color of fabric, the texture of hair, the creases in a cheek when someone smiled.

It was almost like I couldn't recognize the people in my own life. Their faces were there, but it gave me no pleasure to see them. They were just faces. I knew there was a psychological term for emotionally dissociating faces. Some people lived with it for years. I wondered how many people experienced this odd, temporary version. Perhaps emotional shock partially shut down the same parts of the brain that were affected by... Capgras; that's what it was.

I shook myself, recognizing the mental roaming as another form of escape. I kept trying to escape. There had been another time I was desperate to escape. Only I'd spent that time beating a wall into submission. When I'd collapsed afterwards, I'd had my friends, Joseph and Mercy, there to help me, to comfort me and dress my wounds. I didn't have my friends this time.

I choked on a sob and fell to my bed, crying. I didn't want to be alone, and I was so, so alone. I didn't have anyone to talk to, to rely on, to stand up for, or even to hide behind when I was feeling weak. I moaned aloud, keening my grief. I missed my friends. I wanted to see a friendly, trusted face.

Lupé was a friend, but I couldn't tell her all of my secrets. She had voluntarily joined the Center, and I didn't think she would appreciate it if I told her I was really there to steal something from them.

Kaitlyn, too, was a friend, but she was just a woman choosing the Center, much like Lupé. Despite the misgivings I felt that both women had for the center, I couldn't risk trusting them not to blow my cover.

I wanted Joseph, my dearest friend in the world. The person I could tell anything to. We would go months without a word, and it didn't matter. When we needed to talk to each other, there was no reacquainting. We just picked our friendship back up, dusted it off a bit, and kept on going. That's what I loved about him. His love and loyalty were effortless, without conditions.

But Joseph wasn't here, and I didn't want him here. Not because I didn't want him near me, but because I didn't want him to see me like this. For the first time in our friendship, I was deeply ashamed of myself, and I couldn't face him like this.

Then there was Mercy. She wasn't as close as Joseph was, and she was more of a protector. I trusted her completely, but our relationship was more like a business partnership. She was my safety net and, to a certain degree, my guide in the world of heroism.

I could be weak in front of her because compared to her I was already weak in so many ways. She wasn't human. The comparison was irrelevant, illogical. We both knew and accepted that she was stronger, less emotionally vulnerable, less fragile. Like a lion and a mouse.

I could be less than my best self. I could be less than my normal self. I could even be less than anything I'd been in my adult life. She had never been a child, vulnerable to others, bullied physically or emotionally. She had never been a teenager, insecure in her own body, unable to find herself, unsure of her purpose.

Mercy was a creation of the gods, a manifestation of Odin's will. She was divine purpose made flesh. Her body had always been at its prime. Her purpose had always been clear. She had never had reason to doubt herself. So, oddly, it was easier, more comfortable to show those failings to her.

"Mercy, help me, Mercy, please, come help me," I chanted in a hoarse whisper. I lay on my tear-soaked pillow, repeating her name over and over.

She was a god-creature, and gods answered prayers. Surely, given my quest, someone was listening to me. I only hoped she would be able to answer.

"Mercy, help me, Mercy, please." The chanting soothed my mind. My body relaxed, exhausted by my crying. Within minutes, I slipped into a drug-free sleep, the first deep, hard, natural sleep I'd had since arriving at the Center nearly two months ago.

My rest was short-lived. Kaitlyn woke me only a few hours later for the evening meal. I walked with her and Maria to the commons area, feeling their eyes on me. I didn't blame them. I'd been distant and unsteady for weeks, and the two of them had borne the brunt of my failings and my internal struggle.

But I felt different now. I could feel the floor beneath my feet, sort of. Emotions didn't seem so out of reach. I felt more grounded than I had in weeks. Even the display of Zaro's Touch of Peace didn't hold my attention as much as it had before.

I knew I wasn't back to my normal. The longing was there, but it wasn't quite as much of a longing. The feeling of being overwhelmed was still there, but I didn't feel quite as overwhelmed. I had somehow managed to take a first step.

Only, I had no idea what to do next.

CHAPT 18

I told Kaitlyn that I needed to process what she and Maria had talked to me about. It was a weak excuse, but she agreed to take Maria for the night. I hated that Maria gave me a hopeful look that she quickly suppressed. I wanted to be worthy of her faith, but first, I needed to be worthy of my own.

I closed the door to my room, hoping that the time alone would be enough to accomplish what I needed to do. The latch clicked and I leaned my head against the door, sending out a prayer of pure emotion and need. I wasn't sure how to even phrase it, so I didn't bother trying.

"You have returned to us."

"You have come back to our world."

I turned around, hope filling me. The twins stood there, smiling at me. I felt the tears fill my eyes, spilling over my lashes. I smiled and choked out a half laugh, half sob. I covered my mouth to keep from blubbering all over.

I took a deep breath and pulled my hands down so they could hear my whisper, "Thank you for coming."

They both tilted their heads to their left, and spoke in unison, as if stating the completely obvious, "You asked us to."

Before I could respond, a form appeared between them. I recalled that the ravens could create a kind of gateway for gods to travel, and my breath caught as I wondered who I would have to deal with now. If Odin or the Norns showed up, I was pretty sure I'd have a full-on tantrum, dignity be damned.

Instead, a blonde woman in a red flannel shirt, jeans, and hiking boots stepped forward.

"Mercy," I breathed. "Thank the gods."

• • •

It took nearly two hours for me to fully explain everything that had happened. When Mercy realized what kind of diet we had at the center, she'd sent Huginn and Muninn away. By the time they returned, I'd finished telling Mercy everything, including a brief description of my "marriage" to Zaro.

She stood and took a brown paper bag from the ravens and checked its contents. She handed it to me, and I recognized the logo of a fast food chain that specialized in sandwiches piled high with sliced meat.

I took it with a questioning look, but I didn't hesitate to pull out a sandwich and take a huge bite out of it. I moaned as the flavors of the meat hit my tongue with just enough sauce to make it slightly sweet. It took several minutes for me to chew the large chunk of sandwich and swallow since I kept stopping to savor the tastes I'd been missing. When I finally got to the point of eating normally, Mercy explained.

"Meat and protein deprivation can make people more susceptible to manipulation," she said. "Some people can handle a vegan diet by producing the needed vitamins from vegetables and legumes, though it sounds like there isn't much in the way of beans, either. And not everyone produces those nutrients well enough to stay healthy without supplements. So, few beans and no vitamin pills?"

I shook my head, confirming what she said.

"Even in the old days, people knew about this." She shrugged. "Meat was always in high demand in the late winter and early spring, and people would often become angry or despondent until the first big spring hunt."

She noticed I'd finished my sandwich and handed me the bag, gesturing me to take another. I peeked inside and saw two more sandwiches. I grabbed one and unwrapped it.

Mercy continued, "While people didn't have the understanding of nutrients that you do today, and no one forced anyone to eat a diet they didn't want, everyone understood that it was important to have both meat and grains available as much as possible."

She sat down on Maria's bed, watching me. "If you are going to be able to recover your wits and perform at your best, you must have a diet that sustains you." She gestured at the sandwich with a smirk. "While that may not be the healthiest choice of meat, it is a convenient way to get the proteins you've probably been missing."

I nodded, licking my fingers and pulling out the last sandwich. "So, what do I do now?"

Mercy shot me a look. "I don't know," she said, slowly. "I'm not one for strategies, really."

I frowned, remembering our previous adventure. She'd been more helpful then, I was sure. Or maybe she'd been supportive and I'd been more willing to take the lead in deciding what to do.

I shook my head. "I've told you everything," I said. "I just don't have any ideas."

Mercy shrugged. "I'm the confrontational type. I go headlong into battle. But I'm not the one who determines when there is a battle and when there is... anything else." She sighed. "I wish I could be of more help. It sounds like you have a good understanding of what is going on."

I scowled at the remaining half of the sandwich. "Yeah, up close and personal, even."

"That man hurt you in many ways," she said.

I shrugged and picked at the sandwich. Mercy sat back, watching me. We let the silence draw out for several moments.

"Who is to blame?" she asked, quietly.

I wrapped up the rest of the sandwich and tossed it to the side. I shrugged. "I don't know."

Mercy frowned at me. "How can you not know? Don't you feel it in your heart?" She raised her voice with each question until she was nearly yelling at me. "Who do you blame for this?"

"I don't know!" I yelled back. "What kind of a question is that? Who do you think I should blame?"

"It doesn't matter who I think should be blamed," she said coldly. "It matters who you blame."

"But it doesn't," I scowled and crossed my arms. "It doesn't matter who I blame, really, does it?"

Mercy crossed her arms, mimicking my actions. "That kind of depends on who it is, doesn't it? And you aren't answering the question."

I felt frustrated tears building in my eyes. I gritted my teeth against them, angry that she wanted me to answer that stupid question. "Aren't you supposed to be the merciful one? This isn't very merciful."

The blonde woman snorted. "Aren't you supposed to be the hero? This isn't very heroic."

"Not heroic?" I screeched. Did she forget what I just told her? How could she know what I'd been through and say that to me?

"Oh, I'm sorry," Mercy said. "I forgot that you don't want to be the hero, do you?" She paced in front of me. "You are more the logical one, right? But you aren't being very logical about what has happened."

I felt my mouth gaping in shock.

"Or maybe you are the one who has always been willing to delve into the darkness," she said. "Haven't you always been proud of how willing you are to look into the darkest part of your soul?"

"Yes," I mumbled, raising my chin stubbornly. "And I have. I always looked."

Mercy nodded. "Yes, you did," she emphasized the "did."

I narrowed my eyes.

"And you saw that you had a tendency towards violence and rage within you," she continued, her voice softening. "You saw that you didn't always have the love you thought you should for people. You saw anger, frustration and even apathy for others. Isn't that right?"

I nodded, relaxing. I should have known Mercy would understand me. She would be sympathetic towards me now.

She waved her fingers at me. "Oooh, scary!" she said in a mock-spooky voice. "How ever did you manage to face that darkness?"

"It was dark," I protested, barely even noticing the whine in my voice.

"Ha!" she said, throwing her head back mockingly. She pointed her finger at me, advancing closer with each sentence. "The first time you have to deal with real darkness, with a moral confusion that requires you to look at your soul and see tar instead of shadow... The first time you are tested in your conviction to that honesty to yourself, and you just..." she threw her hands up, "lay on your bed. Too morose to even weep. Too lost to your own despair to even face yourself."

"That's not true," I cried, tears falling down my cheeks.

"Lie to yourself," Mercy said, turning away. "But don't lie to me."

She stepped between the twins and disappeared.

I looked at Huginn and Muninn, half expecting them to tell me Mercy had been wrong. Instead, they turned, rotating out until they were back-to-back, fading away as they did so.

I stared at the empty space, confused and unhappy with how Mercy had left me. A pressure was building in my chest, and I knew I was going to cry or get angry. I was tired of crying.

I picked up my pillow and threw it at the wall where the three god-creatures had disappeared. "Fine!" I snarled, jumping to my feet. "You think I won't face the darkness? I'll fucking face it. You can take that judgmental attitude of yours and shove it up your damn Valkyrie ass!" I shook my fist at the wall. "Shove it and twist that shit!"

I paced the room, cussing loudly until I felt myself calming down enough to do the meditation. Somewhere in the back of my mind, I was pleasantly surprised at how long my anger lasted. When I started to relax, I sat down and finished off the last sandwich before grabbing the pillow and settling myself on the floor with my legs crossed.

I took several deep breaths, connecting to the core energy of the earth, reaching with mental tentacles down through the floor, stretching into the ground. I pulled energy up my body through my spine as I breathed in, straightening my back as the energy moved.

I held my breath for a moment, clarifying my intentions and pushing wayward thoughts to the side. I slowly let the breath out, pushing the energy along my limbs, letting it wash off the extra emotions that could block my meditation.

I hesitated a moment, then took the time to focus on each of my chakras. Starting at the base, I visualized each one as a pulsing, spiral galaxy of color. Each one, I noted how fast and strong the light pulsed, how fast the galaxy spun. I narrowed my will into each one, adjusting it until it pulsed and spun at the speed that I somehow knew was right.

Red, orange, yellow, green in my heart, and blue at my throat. Each one set to pulse and spin in sync with the others. The purple in my forehead eased a tension in my mind that I hadn't noticed, and the white just above my skull hovered like a spiral halo around my head.

I didn't often find it necessary to align my chakras, but they had needed the adjustment, and I felt more grounded for it. It was an advantage I would be able to use.

I let my mind drift through recent memories of the energy world. I was taken aback by how few of those memories I had. I hadn't been focused enough on the world around me. Instead, I'd been walking around focused inward, on my own tainted desires and corrupted joys.

I set my jaw, knowing more than ever that this was a step I needed to take. And I stepped into the space of my own mind, visualizing my personal mental existence.

I stood in a lush forest. Each tree represented an event in my own life, and the verdant life around me showed how full my experiences had been. Each tree towered above, but I also knew that the roots stretched far below the earth beneath my feet. I stepped into a tiny clearing among the trees.

The green grass grew thickly except for a section at the center of the clearing. I moved my feet to the edge of the grass, where the green blades gave way to packed brown earth. The bare ground surrounded a gaping hole nearly four feet across. It was so deep that nothing within it was illuminated by the dim forest light.

I stared down at the hole. It was my subconscious mind down there in the darkness. Everything that I didn't let myself know about myself was down there. All the suppressed feelings, dark desires, hidden agendas, and unnamed sins were crawling in those shadows.

I'd stood at the edge of this hole before, several times. It didn't matter. It was familiar, but there was no confidence or comfort in the familiarity. No matter how often I looked into my heart and soul, I found new pain and more secrets to face down.

It was my own mind, but I could never defeat the monsters down there.

I took a deep breath and stepped to the edge of the hole. I straightened my shoulders and clenched my jaw. And I jumped, feet first, into the darkness.

CHAPT 19

I fell into the pitch black darkness.

At first, it was a little jarring, like a jolt of nausea shooting through my gut. But then, I just kept falling. I could feel the air moving around me as I fell. I knew I was moving quickly. If I had reached out, I would have scraped my hand on the walls of the hole that I was falling so quickly through.

After a few minutes, I was bored with falling, and yet I was still falling, like Alice into Wonderland. Except no horrific re-imagining of that place could compare to what I knew was waiting for me. Or what I suspected, at least.

I felt the air change as the tunnel gave way to an enormous cavern, and I knew the falling would stop soon. I landed in a heap on the rock, tumbling sideways when the uneven crust undermined my balance. I felt the rough surface of the rock scrape on my skin.

I was naked. There were no clothes to hide or protect my body in my own mind, after all. I stood up carefully, getting my bare feet stabilized on the graveled surface. I took a few breaths to orient myself in the empty space of the cavern.

I held out my left hand and willed energy into it. A small sphere of cold, blue light appeared, showing me a tiny area of huge rocky mounds set at different heights in the floor of the cavern.

I remembered this, and I nodded. This is how it had to be, then. I began climbing across the stone-studded floor, sliding down to lower rocks, clawing my way up the higher ones. The blue light stayed close to my left shoulder, freeing my hands.

I panted as the unusual exercise went on and on. I paused on one high rock and pushed the blue light up as high as I could, trying to see farther. But the glow only showed the next rock over. I sighed and kept moving.

Rock after endless rock scraped my hands and knees, grating along my shins. My throat was dry and my hair stuck up all over from the wind of my fall and the exertion of my climbing. I leaned for a moment against the latest rock after sliding down it.

I was tired. I didn't want this.

Mercy's words rang out in my mind: *The first time you are tested in your conviction to that honesty to yourself, and you just lay on your bed.*

I frowned and heaved myself up the next steep rock. "Fuck 'em all," I snarled.

A sound roared out in the darkness. I gasped and lost my grip, falling off the rock I was trying to climb. My right foot struck the stone, banging against the toes that were missing in the physical realm. I bit down on my tongue to suppress a cry of pain. A second roar rang through the cave.

I backed up until I was pressed against a stone that rose up just higher than my head. I stared into the darkness. I felt more than heard a movement to my left, and I turned toward it. A scattering of gravel to my right jerked my attention that way.

I heard growling and snarling on the rock behind me, and the fear crept down my legs, turning them to jelly. I fell to my knees and pressed against the rock, holding the light high, desperately trying to see... anything.

As I got used to the constant roaring and snarling, I could hear a voice underneath the bestial sounds. I strained to understand the words, but my attention faltered each time I detected movement in the blackness around me.

I struggled to focus, pulling away from the panic of my fear reactions. I tried to simply acknowledge and accept each movement, each growl, rather than making the effort to know what caused it.

This was a common theme in my Dark Night meditations. I wanted to know. Know what made the noise, know where the creature was, know how it moved, and on and on. But everything here was me. And my fears of the creature were my fears of what I wasn't facing.

It wasn't knowledge that I was lacking. It was acceptance.

So, I tried to accept what was happening. I focused on my breath, breathing through each scattering of gravel, each scrape of claws on stone. I breathed through the flicker of movement to my right, the movement of air behind me. I stopped jumping at every sound and detected motion. I just breathed.

As I relaxed into the fear, accepting the fear without panicking, I heard the voice more clearly. It sounded young, though I knew that the sound itself was only an illusion.

What I was hearing was simply my mind's way of understanding the message. Even though I could hear words, I knew it was just my interpretation of the feelings of accusation that the voice was really projecting.

"Bad, bad, bad, bad," it chanted.

I allowed my thoughts to stretch out, reaching towards the voice. I didn't put words into the thought. I spoke to myself in symbols, feelings, and only sometimes words, and I was dealing with deep, hidden parts of my mind. So I didn't ask a question when I responded, I just sent out the feeling of a question.

"I am bad," the voice said. "You are bad. We are bad."

I sent the feeling of "what" to the voice.

"Noooooooooooooo!" the voice cried, denial slapping at me.

A scaled face lunged at mine, snapping jaws just inches from my nose. The voice snarled at me. "You did this! I did this! We did this!"

I doubled over as feelings of anger and guilt mixed with flashes of memory. I felt the tears falling down my cheeks. The voice was talking about what Zaro had done. What I had let him do.

I looked up as the voice rose in a keening wail. Every sorrow I'd ever experienced was in that sound, and I wept harder, sobbing loudly.

"We allowed this! To us. To them!" the voice cried out in anguish.

I nodded. By not stopping Zaro, I had let him continue using the women in the Center. Not just me.

No. Not using. Abusing.

"You don't know you saved her," the voice bit out, accusingly. Remorse and understanding of my own wretchedness pulled me down, and I saw a face flash through my mind.

I gasped. Lupé. I'd never thought to ask her if my intervention had prevented Zaro from taking her, too. Even though he'd told me it wouldn't.

"I failed! You failed! We failed!"

Despair and hopelessness filled me. The voice howled in pain, and I could hear the creature thrashing itself on the rocks beyond my light. I felt each blow in my mind, like a memory of being beaten.

"You let him!" the voice wailed. "I let him! We let him!"

I lifted my head and let my voice join the keening cry. Feeling the self-hate and shame run through me. I howled out my worthlessness and tore at my own flesh and hair with my fingers. The anguished cries ripped my voice apart, and I finally collapsed, weeping with hoarse moans. The light faded out as my will crumbled.

I heard the creature approach, slithering across the rocks. I struggled to control my breathing. I knew what I had to do, but that didn't make it any easier to do it. Gravel scattered as I scrambled to my feet, stepping on sharp stones in the darkness. I sniffed and tried to stand up straight, but the mourning had left my muscles liquid and unstable.

I closed my eyes and focused on the sound of the creature moving, closer, closer. It felt like it took forever to come within reach, and I held myself still to be sure I wouldn't startle it away. Finally, I could feel the mood shift in the cavern, just a subtle change in the emotional pressure. It was time.

I opened my eyes and called up the light once more. Standing before me was a horrible-looking creature, slimy and scaly, dripping with tangles of long, patchy hair. Spikes stood out along its body in asymmetrical, random places, interspersed with gaping sores that oozed bright yellow-green pus streaked with red blood.

The creature's mouth was skewed to one side, so it looked like a clay model that had fallen on the floor and not been fixed. Teeth of all shapes and sizes jutted out of its jaw at odd angles. Its stubby tail had skin torn off in patches along its length.

One deep red eye sat on top of its head, like the eye of a frog, but with the odd rectangular pupil of a goat. The other eye was pale orange and sat low, to one side of the nose, and seemed to have no pupil at all. It wheezed every breath with a mucousy rattle, and an odor of rotting meat and diseased shit surrounded it, wafting towards me with every micro-gust in the air.

I gulped down the bile that rose at the sight of the creature. It was everything horrible and disgusting in the world. I felt repelled by it at every level of my being. I stared at the creature, willing myself to do what I had to do. There was only one way to be rid of it.

I stepped forward. The creature flinched and snarled, tensing up as if to spring. I hesitated, letting it get used to my new position. It slowly relaxed, and I stepped forward again.

This time, it didn't flinch as much. It watched me with its mismatched eyes and relaxed from its half-crouch. The next step forward, it barely moved, though its eyes flickered from my face to my hands to my feet and back.

I held my hands out, palms forward, slightly away from my body, showing it that I had no weapons. The next step, there was no flinch at all. Instead, the creature made a low moaning noise that sounded like the first part of the sound of vomiting. I forced myself not to cringe at my visceral reaction to the creature's whine. I held the gaze of its sickly orange eye, willing it to stay calm, and I stepped forward again.

I was now inches away from the creature. If either of us moved, we would brush against the other. I tried not to think of the pus and slime coating the matted hair, scales and open sores that covered its body, so close to my bare skin.

I spread my arms wide, and the creature tensed. Before it could react, I stepped forward and wrapped my arms around it. It struggled to get away, thrashing in my arms. It snarled and snapped at my face. Despite its greater size, I was stronger, and I held on tight. The creature whined its vomit-like sound, and I could feel the wetness of pus and slime smearing across my body, dripping down my legs and off my arms. It panted, wheezing and hacking mucus onto my face.

The battle seemed to take hours. Slowly, it weakened, its struggles becoming less intense. I laid my head against its body and began singing a soothing, wordless tune. I felt the body in my embrace shrink in on itself. My hands met behind its back and I cradled the creature, rocking it in my arms. I was covered in the pus and goo, and every breath was a struggle not to gag on the smell. But I sang to the creature, and I pushed love energy through my arms towards it. And I cuddled it as it shrank down.

I lost track of time, and it seemed sudden when the change happened. In a blink, I was no longer rocking the shrunken body of a filthy beast. Instead, my arms held a little girl of about three or four years old.

She was naked, like me, and her body was covered in gashes and deep purple and yellow bruises. Scars crisscrossed her skin and her dark hair was tangled and matted. Her voice croaked with sobs as she cried out her pain in my arms. I rocked her and sang to her, patting her back gently and stroking her hair, sending love from my heart to hers.

Eventually, her crying stopped and she slowly sat up. I smiled at her and wiped the tears from her cheeks. I pushed at my will to soothe the bruises and cuts from her face.

I waved my arm, and there was a shallow hot spring, glowing with a golden healing light. I led her to it and picked up the soft cloths at the side of the pool. I eased us both into the water and bathed her, gently, carefully, soothing away her wounds with the magic of love in my heart and with my will.

When we were cleaned off all the remnants of the creature she had been, I sat her in front of me and combed out her hair, singing a song that we remembered from another life. Clean, combed and dry, I wrapped her in a warm blanket and held her close. Then I began to speak, with words and with the language of emotions and memories.

"I'm sorry," I said, softly. "I failed you. I failed Ella and Maria. I failed Lupé and so many others.

"I'm so sorry, but I am also not the only one who failed. I am not the only one who harmed others. I will take responsibility for my failings. I will make reparations to the best of my ability. But I will not take on the burden of other people's guilt. I will not take responsibility for other people's actions."

I squeezed the girl who was both my own inner child and the embodiment of my faults and weaknesses, abused by the hurts that had been visited on me and the hurts I had visited on others, and I loved her without judgment. I held her and accepted what both what I had done and what had been done to me.

As the child fell asleep, I took a deep breath. Accepting what had been done didn't mean forgiving or forgetting. It didn't mean pretending it had never happened or walking away without demanding restitution. It didn't mean I wouldn't make Zaro pay for what he'd done.

CHAPT 20

I blinked at the bright light in my eyes.

I wasn't sure where I was, but I was extremely uncomfortable, yet I didn't want to move. I took a deep breath and realized I was lying on the floor on my side.

I peered at the blinding yellow light and realized it was the sun shining through the little window in my room at the Center. I frowned. I knew I'd always had the window, but I didn't remember ever noticing the sunlight shining through it before.

I thought about getting up and moving somewhere more comfortable, but the sunlight was warm on my face, and I felt it seeping inside me, brightening up the corners of my mind. I closed my eyes and smiled softly, indulging in the warmth.

The door creaked softly, and I heard a soft shuffle of feet. I moved my head toward the sound and opened my eyes. Two pairs of feet stood only half a foot from my face. The smaller feet were bare and pale under a cream linen dress. The larger feet behind them peaked out, ebony skin under the pale hem of loose pants and crisscrossed with beige rope sandal straps.

I grinned and scrambled upright. My hip was sore from pressing into the floor, but I ignored it as I pulled myself to my feet. I saw the cautious looks on their faces.

"Maria! Kaitlyn!" I said, unable to contain my happiness that they were there. After the encounter with my own subconscious, I needed to start rebuilding everything that I'd let fall apart. Starting with the trust I'd lost with these two. "I am so glad to see you!"

I realized it would be too fast to try to hug Maria, but I didn't know what else to do. I felt suddenly awkward and unsure about talking to them. I knew it was partially due to my own fears that they would reject my attempts to recover our relationships.

I took a deep breath and sat on the bed, gesturing for Maria and Kaitlyn to sit down as well. "I owe you both an apology."

Kaitlyn sat on Maria's bed and the girl followed her, holding onto the woman's arm. They both watched me closely, but let me speak.

"Maria, you were right about what I was doing," I said. "You were right to be upset with me, and you were right to be unhappy with my behavior."

I paused, trying to get my thoughts organized. "I let you down, and I would like to think that I won't do it again, but I have to be honest. I found out that I'm not as strong as I once thought I was."

I felt my self-control slipping as I thought about how I'd emotionally abandoned the girl. I pressed my lips together for a moment, trying to hold the emotions in check until I could get the words out.

"I don't know that I won't make you feel left behind again," I croaked. "But I can promise I will not forget what has happened, and I will not ignore how we have all been hurt."

I took a shaky breath. "I can't make you believe me, but I still want you to know that I... understand things better than I did yesterday."

Maria stared at me with her eyes wide. She nodded, and I hoped she understood what I was trying to say to her.

I lifted my gaze to Kaitlyn's dark eyes and swallowed hard. "And you, Kaitlyn," I said. "You have been a better friend than I have deserved. You took on the responsibilities that I let slide." I glanced at Maria and sighed.

"I have been lost," I continued, forcing the words out around my pride. "You could have given up on me, but instead..."

I shook my head. "Instead, you confronted me with my truth. You shined a light on my behavior when I would have let it fester in the dark."

I pressed my lips together for a moment, closing my eyes against the shame that I felt. "You don't know how much you've done to save me." I looked up at her, searching her face for a sign that she believed me. "I can never repay you for that. I can only try to live my life better now."

I let the words fade into silence. I watched the woman and the girl, and they watched me. We all seemed to be searching for hope, but it was still too early to see it for sure.

Kaitlyn cleared her throat. "So, what does this mean? What is going to change?"

I shrugged. "It's hard to say," I admitted. "I came here for a reason, and that is still something I need to follow through with. I can't just leave, though that would be best for me."

Maria gasped. "No!" She slipped out of Kaitlyn's arm and ran up to me. "Please, don't make me go back to Roger!"

"I won't, honey." I reached out to her and let her fall into my arms. "No matter what happens, I won't make you go back to that man."

I waited until she had calmed a little, then I lifted her up to look her in the eye. "I will find a way to help you, but we have to do this the right way." I made sure I had her attention, catching her eye. "We have to help your mother so she can come back to you, or to legally let you go."

Maria's face screwed up and she cried. I held her and stroked her hair. The whole situation sucked, and it wasn't fair that this little girl was caught up in something that was made complicated by the laws and rules meant to protect her.

I caught Kaitlyn's eye over Maria's shoulder. She was frowning but she nodded. I could tell by her expression that she understood the issues of custody and how that could make the right thing nearly impossible. It was a sad situation.

Maria eventually cried out her fears and soon was sitting next to me with my arm around her thin body. I waited to see where the two of them would take this discussion next.

Finally, Kaitlyn spoke up again. "You have to stay, but you say things have changed," she said in her low silky voice. "I guess I don't know why we should believe you."

I nodded. "Fair point. You don't." I shrugged. "I was... addicted, for lack of a better word. That's what Zaro does to people, particularly women. He feeds them – us – this emotional drug and we get high. We want more."

"And now?" she asked.

"Now," I said, setting my jaw. "Now, I've seen what's happened to me. And it pisses me off. I'm pissed at Zaro. I'm pissed at myself. And

I'm disappointed in myself." My head dropped down as I shook it.

"Why are you disappointed in yourself?" Kaitlyn asked. "If this guy has been drugging you in some way, could you have fought him off? I mean, does he give you a pill or something?"

I sighed. I should have realized that Kaitlyn would latch on to a real-world reason for the addiction. I could tell that was how she saw the world – real, physical problems with real, physical solutions. I tried to think of how to explain the energy addiction to her.

"It's not a pill," I began. "It's not even a physical drug..." I trailed off, not sure what to say.

"So a device that gives off some kind of signal, like a sub-harmonic or something?" she suggested. She ignored me when I started shaking my head. "He's always grabbing that pendant when he does the thing after supper."

I froze.

Zaro paused, laying his body across mine and pinning me down. He reached for his neck and grasped the wire pendant with his right hand while stroking my face with his left. My eyes rolled back with the taste of rich tiramisu gliding down my throat.

He had grabbed his pendant. I forced myself to remember each encounter with Zaro, each time he'd raped me. He always clutched the pendant and then the feeling would wash over me stronger.

The feeling of warmth, of contentment, of simple pleasures... the feeling of comfort. I knew that power.

It was written in the words of Odin, in the Havamal, which laid out Odin's rules and experiences in Midgard, the human world. It was written in the stanzas that explained the magicks that Odin gained in exchange for his eye at the Well of Mimir, the seer, at the hands of the Norns.

The Runespells.

I thought it out. The strength of the energy, the consistency of its effects, the way he held the pendant, kept it against his skin.

It made sense. Zaro had one of the Runespells.

I nodded to myself, then I blinked, realizing that Kaitlyn was watching me. I cleared my throat and wracked my brain for what she had said to me.

"I think you're right," I said. "He must be using some device on us."

She nodded. "Well, then, you shouldn't be so hard on yourself. You had no way to defend against it, right?"

I shrugged, unwilling to fully agree with her. She didn't know we were still talking about energy, but I still felt that my years of experience as an energy worker, as a witch, should have counted for something. But then again, the Runespells were literally the spells of the gods turned into magical pendants. Could I really have stood a chance against that, even if I'd been prepared? I just didn't know for sure.

"I'm still disappointed in myself," I muttered stubbornly. "Whether I deserve to be or not."

Kaitlyn stared at me for a moment and nodded. "Alright, then," she said. "That's what has convinced me."

I looked at her.

She grinned. "People who tend to feel like you do, are also the ones who step up and take responsibility," she explained. "You aren't willing to give up all the blame, even if it could be justified. You own what you've done, even if it's not your fault you did it."

She sat back and stared at me, her face suddenly serious. "Maybe I'll be able to trust you, after all," she murmured. Then she sat up, slapped her hands on her legs and stood up. "If we sit around here any longer, we won't get our breakfast."

She reached out to take Maria's hand. "And it's the most important meal of the day."

I snorted. "What you mean is, we don't eat enough to miss any meals, right?"

Maria smiled and held both our hands as we walked to the commons area.

I let myself relax just a little. I'd begun rebuilding bridges, and I'd located, not one, but two Runespells. But I was nowhere near the end of my trials here. Whoever said that knowing was halfway there, had never been a hero sent on an epic quest.

Plus, I still needed to face Mercy, and I had no idea how she was going to react to me this time.

CHAPT 21

I hadn't realized how hard it would be to keep up the facade of still being an obedient Hand in the Center and entranced wife to Zaro.

I moved through the day, eating breakfast, watching Zaro perform his workshop, checking on Maria, working my gardening shift, interacting with the other Hands. I found myself gaping at things in shock that I'd never noticed before. What I'd been missing was too often horrible.

I watched one of the men groping one of Zaro's wives. He'd made a comment to another guy that "if you don't mind sloppy seconds, you can take whatever you want from them after they visit Zaro's room."

I clenched my hands into fists when he took the unresisting woman behind a shed. Anger filled me and I struggled to control myself until I realized that I might very well have been taken behind a shed, too. I simply couldn't remember.

I turned from the scene with bitter tears filling my eyes. I focused on my breathing, promising myself that this would end. I noticed Kaitlyn watching me sadly. Her jaw clenched when she glanced at the man still leaning on the shed while his friend took what he wanted. She was as frustrated by the situation as I was.

It was an exercise in self-control. I couldn't believe I'd never noticed all the wrongs going on under my nose. It hit me how out of it I'd been, even from the first day. I felt a burning shame for having dropped the ball so severely.

I lavished attention on Maria, the only person I could save at the moment. I even gave her a bit of extra food from my own plate. I was hungry again, ravenously so, but I hoped I could get the ravens and Mercy to help me with that again.

As soon as I thought it, I edged away from the idea. I still wasn't looking forward to my next encounter with Mercy. She'd been so harsh last time, I was afraid it was an indication of how our relationship had permanently changed.

I admitted to myself that I had needed the push that her dismissive exit had given me. I hoped it was the case that she'd done it intentionally for that reason. If she hadn't, if that was really how she felt about me...

I wondered if I would be assigned another Valkyrie or something.

Maria tugged at my sleeve, getting my attention. I bent down to talk to her quietly, but she just watched me with huge eyes. It took me a minute to realize that I'd been lost in thought, and it had probably looked like I'd slipped back into my previous behaviors.

I smiled at her and squeezed her reassuringly. The meal had ended and Zaro was showing off his power with another young girl on stage. But I didn't feel desire for what he was doing. I didn't feel jealous of the girl, and I didn't have to fight the urge to rush the stage to beg the man for the gift of his Touch.

Instead, I felt sad that so many people, including myself, had fallen under his influence. And I renewed my promise to myself that I would do whatever I could to end it, once and for all.

I took my time with Maria that night, telling her Ella's favorite bedtime story to the best of my memory and tucking her in with many reassurances. I couldn't promise I wasn't going to go to the astral plane tonight. I might need to go to get a hold of the ravens. And I wasn't sure that Maria had even realized that extent of my escapism.

I did promise her I'd be there for her if she needed me, all night and in the morning, too. I could do that, no matter how the evening went.

As the girl's snores started filling the room, I sat on my bed, waiting and hoping for visitors. I started to doze off in the dim light and the silence of the night.

"Is she sleeping?"

"Or is she astral?"

I started awake at the twin voices. I blinked up at the ravens in their human form and smiled.

"Neither," I mumbled and stretched, still sitting on the bed.

The two grinned and the air shimmered between them. Mercy's

blonde head appeared, looking stern as she stepped out of the space between the ravens.

"Mercy," I said, nodding a greeting. "I'm glad you came back tonight."

She raised an eyebrow as if to question my statement. She turned and looked at the sleeping girl in the other bed before she set her feet, standing near the dresser. She crossed her arms, waiting.

I smiled wryly. She wasn't going to make this easy on me, not that she should. Given my recent situation, I didn't blame her, though it would have been easier if she had just forgiven me and we could go back to how it was before.

I sighed. That was part of the consequences of my behavior. I was pretty firm with Ella about having to suffer consequences, but it wasn't fun or easy or anything. That's what made living the proof of one's changed behaviors so important – it was hard to do.

"First of all," I began, "I need to thank you for what you said last night." I looked down at my hands. "I needed to hear what you said. I needed to... not be coddled."

I looked up at her. She seemed more relaxed now.

I continued before my emotions got the better of me. "I want you to know that I did it," I said. "I looked into my own subconscious, my own soul."

Mercy nodded. "And?"

I swallowed at the memory. "It was really hard," I admitted, looked down at the floor. I couldn't say what I had to say while looking at the Valkyrie's eyes. "I almost couldn't follow through. I don't remember it being that hard before." I ran my hand through my hair. "But I faced some things. I admitted some things. And I accepted... shit, a lot of things. Mostly I accepted my own responsibility."

I glanced up and she smiled softly. I returned the smile before pressing my lips together. I wasn't done.

"I also made an oath," I said.

Mercy froze, the smile falling from her face. "What kind of oath, Nicola?"

I raised my chin. "I made an oath to fix this," I waved my hand indicating the center, "and put a stop to Zaro and Nancy."

Mercy frowned and stepped forward. "That's not your

responsibility."

I shook my head. "No, it isn't. But I haven't done enough, and it needs to be done." I locked my eyes onto hers. "There's more."

Mercy tilted her head and waited.

"I've discovered both Runespells-"

"Both?" she blurted.

"-and Bob," I finished.

Mercy's head jerked as she recoiled. I caught the movement of the raven's heads swinging towards me, too.

"Are you sure?" the Valkyrie whispered. "We haven't heard anything about him since..."

"I'm sure," I bit out. "And he needs to be dealt with." I pulled my feet up to cross them as I sat on the bed. "I'm not playing around anymore, Mercy. I won't be screwing around with the same stupid bad guy over and over." I shot her a determined look. "I'm not going to be that overly righteous hero that doesn't pull the damn trigger."

Mercy leaned back against the dresser, crossing her arms and staring at the floor. I let the silence stretch out. I figured she needed a moment to process all the information I'd just given her.

After a few minutes, I glanced over at the ravens. "Hey, guys?" They looked at me and I shot them a super-sweet smile. "Don't suppose you got any more of them meaty sandwiches, huh?"

The twins grinned at me and nodded to me and then Mercy before disappearing.

I turned back to Mercy. "I think the extra food is helping me stay focused. So, thank you for that."

She nodded. "You said 'both' Runespells. You think there are two?"

"Yeah," I said. "The healing one is a bit obvious, in retrospect, and I'm certain it's in the Rod of Asclepius – that scepter thing that we use during the Selection and that Nancy uses during the Healing itself. I just have to figure out how to find it."

"And the other?"

"I'm convinced that Zaro is using the First Runespell to control the members here and to..." I choked on the words. "He rapes women and calls them his wives. They can't resist him because of the... the feelings he pushes on them... during."

Mercy frowned. "Are you sure?"

I nodded.

"The first Runespell..." she said. "I guess it could be used like that. I don't know anyone who would even think of doing that, though. Maybe your source was mistaken. Who told you about this?"

I looked down at my hands. "I didn't need to be told."

"Then how do you know?"

I looked up at Mercy and stared at her. Understanding spread across her face, but I said it anyways, biting out the words. "First-hand experience."

"Odin's Left Eye!" she gasped. "I had no idea that... I knew about the food and the trials, but... Oh, Nicola!"

I flinched when she moved towards me, certain she was going to hug me and try to comfort me, or something. I had worked so hard at getting my power back, being comforted like a child wasn't what I wanted.

Instead, she dropped to one knee in front of me, bowing her head.

I gaped at her for a moment. "Wh-what are you doing?"

Mercy raised her head. "I had no idea that you'd overcome so much. And you did so with only a nudge from the rest of us. Your power, your will is what has saved you. And I knew so little about what your battle was." She raised her right fist over her heart. "I can think of no other way to honor the warrior that you are."

I bit my lip, unsure of what to do with the Valkyrie's gesture. She stood up and went back to leaning against the dresser as the ravens reappeared.

I grinned. They had a paper bag with them.

CHAPT 22

Mercy and I chatted for a few hours, going over details and possibilities while I munched on the sandwiches that the twins had brought me. While we didn't really reach any conclusions about what to do, I felt infinitely better about being able to deal with whatever came up.

I went to sleep without any urge to go into the astral realm, though I realized I hadn't told Mercy about Jehovah, and I knew I'd have to confront the god eventually.

Instead, I let myself sleep deeply and I woke in the morning with more energy than I'd thought I could have at this point. Maria seemed happy that I'd been so involved with her the last previous day, and I hoped I would be able to continue being there for her.

• • •

I snuck up to the fourth floor, trying to get more information about Nancy's habits. She was the type of person who stayed on task and on schedule, so I figured I'd be able to map out her patterns and use that to sneak in and grab the Rod.

Nancy walked around the floor, checking in on the patients every hour on the half-hour. She always saved Bob for last, and she spent the most time in his room. Then she sat at the desk in the center of the floor and wrote notes in her charts.

It was boring and pretty much useless. The woman was nearly always around during the day. I realized I'd have to try late at night.

I had been crouched in the stairwell for several hours, fighting anxiety every time someone climbed up to the third floor. If they saw me, or if they continued up to the fourth floor, I'd be caught with no good reason to be there.

I shook my head at the wasted time and peered over the rail to check for people below. I tiptoed down to the landing between the third and fourth floors and froze at the sight of someone coming up the steps to the third floor landing.

"Shit!" I gasped. "Kaitlyn, you scared the crap out of me!"

The woman clutched the rail with one hand, the other over her heart, as she eyed me. "Same to you!" she whispered. She took two more steps up. "What are you doing?" Her gaze moved up the stairs to the fourth floor landing, where I'd just come from. "Were you up there?"

I waved her into silence. "Shhh!"

I searched her face, trying to decide if I could trust her with my secrets. I took a deep breath when I realized I hadn't been trusting my own instincts for too long. My gut said to trust her.

I stepped down to meet her and touched her arm. "We need to talk," I said. "I need to be honest with you."

Kaitlyn nodded and we walked down the stairs. She kept glancing at me nervously. I understood. I just hoped neither one of us was going to regret this. I pulled Kaitlyn into my room. I glanced at the clock and realized we only had a little time before we would have to go to supper, and I needed to go find Maria in the gardens before then.

I looked at Kaitlyn. "I'm going to trust you, and I'm going to tell you this quickly, so... "

She searched my face, then nodded slowly. "Alright, then."

I considered where to start. "Once upon a time," I said. "I was given a... job. To collect these... devices. That's why I'm here. One of these... devices is being used for the healing ceremonies."

Kaitlyn frowned. "What kind of device? Like what we were talking about with Zaro?"

I nodded. "Something like that, yeah." I sighed. "Look, this is going to sound crazy, but... they are magic pendants created by the Norse god, Odin, and they have been given to various people to start the end of the world." I rushed the words out and then waited for Kaitlyn's response.

She stared at me. "You tried that line before. What kinda crazy do you take me for anyways?"

She started to push past me to leave, and I grabbed her arm.

"Will you at least let me try to prove it?" I challenged.

Kaitlyn hesitated. "You think you can prove this? Fine."

I turned to the dresser and dug through the few personal items I'd kept with me. I pulled out the lighter and handed it to her.

"Light it and keep it lit," I said.

She hesitated and I nodded to encourage her. She flicked the lighter and a small flame jumped up. I pressed my hand against the pendants under my shirt. One of them grew warm as I drew on its power.

I held my other hand over the flame.

Kaitlyn frowned. "Honey, this is high school tricks..."

I drew the flame up, branching it into two streams of fire. I lowered my hand down and the branches arched around my fingers and came back together above them.

"Holy mother Yemaya!" Kaitlyn whispered.

I glanced at her and smiled. I pulled my hand out of the circle of flame and let the fire return to a single pillar, six inches long. I moved my hand over it, bending the flame sideways into a ninety-degree angle as my flesh passed over it.

Kaitlyn gasped as she stared at the fire that was very obviously breaking laws of physics. I pulled my hand away from the fire and took the lighter from her. I put it away, then faced her, crossing my arms and raising one eyebrow.

She stared at me for a moment. "How did you do that?"

I shrugged. "I have a few of these magic pendants," I admitted. "But they haven't been very helpful up 'til now." Then I smirked and caught her eye. "'Holy mother Yemaya'?" I gave her a questioning look. "You said you were into Voodoo?"

Kaitlyn pressed her lips together. "Santeria, actually."

"And you follow Yemaya?"

Kaitlyn stared at me.

"I'm Pagan, remember," I said. "We tend towards energy work and lots of knowledge about lots of religions."

She nodded slowly. I watched her pace back and forth for a moment, lost in thought, then she turned back to me. "Is that why you were so adamant that you should have been able to resist Zaro's...

whatever he has?"

I nodded. "He's got a pendant, like mine. But where mine lets me control fire, to a point, his lets him give people comfort and peace."

"Peace?" Kaitlyn frowned. "That's what he does to the women?"

I nodded. "Now, I have to get both Runespells, both pendants, from Nancy and Zaro, but I can't figure out how to get to them."

Kaitlyn frowned. "What do you need? Help or what?"

I shrugged. "I don't know. Everything is so rigid." I sighed. "Maybe a rebellious uprising, or at least a loud distraction."

Kaitlyn bit her lip and stared at me.

"I don't know," I admitted. I glanced at the clock again. "We better get going," I said. "Maybe you can help me think of something...?"

Kaitlyn hesitated, then nodded. "I'll do whatever I can to stop the abuses here."

She hurried out the door, and I followed behind.

CHAPT 23

After two days, I began to suspect that Kaitlyn was avoiding me. We went through our days, but she managed to finish her meals when I brought Maria to eat, and she always had somewhere to be. So she apologized and disappeared until the next meal.

On the fourth day, I was convinced she was avoiding me. I considered tracking her down and asking her to explain, but I decided she must have a reason for her actions.

I knew, deep down, that Kaitlyn was a good and honorable woman. I just had to believe there was a reason for what she was doing. I had to believe that I'd been right to trust my instincts. Instead of forcing Kaitlyn's hand, I focused on gathering information. I volunteered to help with the Selection, and I found out that the Rod was kept in a strong box in between the Selection and Healing ceremonies.

I tried to learn where the strong box was, exactly, but I found Nancy staring at me too often, so I had to be more circumspect in my search. If the woman moved the Rod before I could get to it, all my efforts would be for nothing.

I could feel myself floundering. I had new purpose but no direction. My frustration grew every day, and I found myself snapping at people for no reason. I needed guidance, but there was no one who could just show up and give it to me. And I still wasn't ready to go back to the astral plane. I still needed distance from the temptation of escape.

Whenever someone asked me for advice on how to find direction, I had several standard suggestions.

First was a form of divination – Tarot cards, runes, pendulums. All of them were ways to tap into universal knowledge. The idea was that everyone already had the information they needed, they just needed it brought out in a way that wasn't loaded down with emotions and biases. But I didn't have my Tarot or runes, and the situation seemed too complex for the yes or no responses of a pendulum.

The second was to ask spirit guides for help. They were best found in the astral plane, so I didn't really want to do that unless I was out of options.

Lastly, I suggested a meditation or vision quest. They were easy to do, once you knew how, but they were harder to understand. Visions are heavily cloaked in metaphor, so it could take a while to understand what they meant. But I had an advantage. I'd already done a vision. I just needed to figure out the underlying meaning.

That evening, after I put Maria to bed, I sat cross-legged on my own bed and closed my eyes. I breathed deeply, clearing my mind. All of the thoughts of the day drifted off on mists that I created.

My mind cleared, I let myself float in the darkness of my own empty psyche for a long time. It had been a long time since I'd allowed myself to feel the peace of the universal connection that came from just being, without thoughts intruding on the act of feeling. I relished the sense of balance I'd been missing for so long.

Once I felt centered within myself, I pulled up the memory of my previous vision. I skimmed through the cave and went to the treasure-filled cavern. I scanned the room, noting the various treasures – a jeweled sword, gold bands, silver tiaras, coins of all shapes and sizes. While the treasures were diverse, they were not what I was looking for. I moved on to the chests.

The first chest was the box of cream fabric with lace and tulle accents. I remembered pulling out the picture, the one I couldn't see clearly. I looked carefully at the frame, a rich gold-leafed wood that struck a chord in my mind.

The image itself appeared to be of three people in front of a green background of some kind, but that was all I could make out. I reviewed the bit of memory several times, but I couldn't make the picture become clear. However, I noticed a small crack in the glass covering the image. The crack cut between one of the people and the other two.

The second chest was the crystalline box containing the jade statue of the two-in-one man. My memory of the statue was clear, and I was certain it was a representation of Satan and Jehovah. I tried to imagine one of the faces of the man as a living person. I visualized the mouth moving, the face giving a smug grin, and my breath caught. Definitely Satan.

I switched to the other face and pictured it in a variety of expressions and imagined it with a beard that would make old rock bands ashamed. And I saw the face I knew. Jehovah. I nodded in confirmation of my suspicions, but I would have to deal with that whole issue later.

I moved on to the third chest, the wooden chest covered with seaweed. The doll with dark hair was an old-fashioned style, with only suggested facial features and no fingers or toes. The dress was a classic design – knee-length with cap sleeves, the fabric in a floral pattern. There was nothing particularly special about the doll.

But I remembered a two year old girl wearing a dress that looked just like it. Her hair was the same dark color as she twirled with the ungainly balance of a toddler. Her giggles drifted through my mind, and I smiled even as my eyes burned with tears.

Ella.

I clutched the memory of the doll to my chest, wishing I could hold my daughter in my arms the same way. But she was with my mother, far from this horrible place and its horrible events. She couldn't be touched by the evils I'd found here.

The fourth chest was the smaller metal box. In my memory, I traced the symbols burned into the leather straps that bound it closed. They were an intricate design, and very artistic, but I'd never seen any symbols like them.

This box held the key. It seemed like an unusual key, with several square teeth instead of the more modern triangular or slightly curved bitings. One of the teeth even came out in a slightly T-shaped bump.

I turned the key over, looking at the symbols. They seemed familiar, so I rotated the key in my mind, trying to match them to some bit of knowledge buried in my memories. The symbols were made with a series of straight lines, crossing over each other.

One of the symbols caught my eye, and I focused on it for a moment. I scowled, trying to understand why it made me think of

141

knives. No, not knives. Blades. The bindrune for the Third Runespell, which prevented injury from blades and other sharp edges.

As that realization sunk in, the others clarified into other bindrunes, eighteen in total. I recognized the four I'd already gotten, but the others all had the same look to them. This key was related to the Runespells in some way.

I moved on to the last chest, the small marble sarcophagus with the bones of a child. I stared at the skeleton for a long time, once again feeling an intense sorrow over it. I couldn't see anything about the bones that would give a hint to who it was, except for the beaded bracelet.

I recalled picking up the arm and grasping the bracelet, and I replayed that section of memory over. I looked closely at the beads and realized they were alternating heads of bears and panthers. No one I knew had an affinity for bears or panthers, or even made me think of bears or panthers.

I went back in my memory a bit to where I had looked into the box. I had noticed the dirt on the bottom of the chest. I stared at it, but I couldn't tell if there was a forensic point to it. It looked like dirt, just like the dirt around my own home.

I sighed.

I knew I'd been at the memory analysis for quite a while, and I felt like I'd gotten everything I could out of it for now. I let the memories go and quickly came back to my physical body. I groaned and stretched before glancing at the clock. I'd been under for several hours. I sighed, knowing I had found out enough to know what I needed. And none of it would be easy.

• • •

It was late when I walked down the quiet hallway to the large women's restroom facilities and went into my usual stall. On the opposite side of the large room, separated by the sinks, there were five small shower stalls, which people used throughout the day for their daily bathing.

Cleaning the bathrooms was a shared chore, and one that was assigned to those who seemed to be potential troublemakers in the Center, so I was surprised I'd never been assigned the job. I didn't care for cleaning toilets or showers.

I sat down to do my business and I heard someone enter the bathroom. In the tradition of women everywhere who'd suffered through bullying in high school, I froze, holding my breath and my bladder. The other woman moved around for a few moments, then I heard one of the showers turn on. I let out my breath and quickly finished my business.

I moved to the sinks to wash my hands and glanced over at the showers. There were benches between the showers and the sink area, and I noticed the pile of clothes on one of them.

My breath caught in my throat. The clothes piled up were white cotton, not the cream and tan linen that most of us wore. And the shoes were pure white sneakers instead of the rope sandals. Nancy was in the shower.

A metallic glint caught my eye and I looked closer. It was her keychain, filled with at least a dozen keys. One of those had to be the key for the strong box that contained the Rod.

I glanced up at the shower and considered my options. The Healing for the week was already done, and the Selection was still two days away. If I could find the right key, I would have nearly forty-eight hours to get to the box and steal the Runespell.

Big if.

I gently pulled the keys out from the pocket they were tucked into. So many keys. How would I ever figure out the right one?

Then I noticed that one of the keys had a different look than the others. The teeth were more square-shaped, and one of them had an extra bit that made it into a kind of T.

Just like the key in my vision.

I grabbed the keys, holding them tightly so they wouldn't clink together. I worked at the key ring, prying it open with my fingernails to move the key around it and off. It took me several minutes to do so, glancing up at the shower every few seconds. My stomach clenched with the fear of being caught.

Finally, the key fell off the ring and I dropped the rest of the keys gently back onto the pile of clothing. The shower stopped and I jumped. Clenching the key in my fist, I bolted for the door.

My heart was still pounding hard when I got back to my room. I tried to calm my breathing as I stared down at the key in my hand. Then I grinned. After all this time, the damn thing practically fell into my lap.

But where to keep it?

If I left it hidden in my dresser drawer, I wouldn't have it on me if I got an opportunity to get to the strong box. If I kept it in the pocket of my loose pants, it could fall out, and I was paranoid enough to believe it would.

I lay back on my bed, turning the key over in my hands. I felt the chain around my neck slide as I reclined. I pulled it away from my throat, feeling the Runespells that were strung onto it.

It was amazing that no one had ever commented on the chain or the pendants. Even Zaro had never seemed to notice it. I frowned. He should have at least recognized the Runespells as being similar to the charms that he was using.

I wondered if it wasn't part of the magic of the chain itself. It was, after all, a very powerful magic item. I lifted the chain and looked at it. It was a thin silver strand, but it was stronger than any steel cable. A piece of Gleipnir, the dwarven-made chain was created to bind Fenrir, the monstrous wolf-son of Loki. It was made of impossible things, like the sound of a cat's footstep and the breath of a fish, and it was the only thing in the Nine Worlds that could hold the wolf-creature.

It had been given to me with a note: "Accept this gift – a piece of the chain of the Wolf. It cannot be broken nor removed but by the wearer." When I placed the Runespells against it, they somehow attached themselves to the chain, making them virtually impossible to steal unless I voluntarily took the necklace off.

I sat up, gears turning in my mind. Maybe...

I held the chain up in one hand and laid the key against it. I held my breath, waiting several long seconds.

Finally, the chain appeared to melt around the key for a split second, and the key was attached.

Then I frowned. I might need to get the key back to Nancy, if the timing wasn't right. Otherwise, I could lose any chance of getting to the Rod. I pulled on the key, wanting it to come back off the chain, and suddenly it did.

I grinned and reattached the key, thrilled that things were starting to go right. Now I just had to find the strong box and get the Runespell out of the Rod without alerting anyone to what had happened so that I would have time to confront Zaro and take his pendant. Then, I would just have to find a way to get out of this place, preferably with Maria and even Kaitlyn, and let the authorities know about the abuses going on.

No problem.

CHAPT 24

I collapsed on my bed, exhausted from spending the entire day on edge. Since I'd snatched the key from Nancy the night before, I'd been hyper-alert, searching for opportunities to look for the strong box.

I'd even sneaked up to the fourth floor when the nurse was on her lunch break, digging through the boxes of files under the central desk.

Nothing. I'd hit a dead-end. I needed to be struck by inspiration.

Unfortunately, the pressure of finding the box wasn't the only thing on my mind. I kept thinking back to the jade statue. I knew what it meant, but I wasn't thrilled with the conclusions I was reaching because of that. I didn't like what it meant for everything that I'd learned about the Runespells.

I didn't like what it meant about Keith, and Bob.

I let out a deep breath. I knew what I needed to do. I had to face the one being that I'd been afraid to confront since the realization had hit me. But I was afraid. He was much more powerful than I could ever hope to be, and it was something that I wasn't entirely sure I would be able to live through.

My vision had indicated that I needed to do this, though. So I shrugged to myself and muttered, "Today is a good day to die."

I entered the astral plane, noting how much easier it was to do so now than it had been a few months ago. I shook my head. Practice makes perfect, and I'd had way too much practice.

I looked around at my surroundings. The first thing I noticed is that it didn't have the too-green, slightly slimy look that it had taken on during my psychic fugue. There were no shadows following me, feeding off of my distress.

My mind was no longer rotting from the inside, and the energies of the astral plane reflected that. I took a deep breath, relieved that the astral plane had confirmed my recovery.

I moved around for a while, determined to prove to myself that my addiction was over by staying just a bit longer than absolutely necessary. If I let the fear of my previous weakness take hold, then I would flee from the astral plane just as I'd fled into it before. Neither would be to my advantage in the long run. I needed to be able to use the astral plane, just as I had before, without fear and without addiction.

After I'd drifted around, checking out a few of my favorite locations, I decided it was time. I took a deep breath and tried not to be too terrified. After all, I'd faced down a god before, though Odin had good reasons to not be inclined to murder me on the spot. This was... very different.

I closed my eyes, swallowed hard, and focused on the garden of Jehovah. The world tilted around me and I knew, before I'd even opened my eyes, that I wasn't alone. I took a shaky breath and faced the god.

Jehovah's eyes were still bracketed by laugh lines, but there was no hint of a pleasant expression. He glared at me, and I could feel the anger radiating off of him.

"What do you want?" he demanded, his voice low and calm but clipped. "I did not bring you here."

I fell back on my old habits. I leaned on one hip and shrugged. "I figured I'd just stop by and see how an old friend was doing."

The god stared at me, eyes narrow.

I took that as a sign that he wasn't going to strike me down... yet. "See, you and I go back some, don't we?" I shot him a saucy grin. "About, what? Eight, nine months now?"

He watched me.

I shrugged. "We've had our differences, sure, but that's not a thing, right?"

He scowled.

"Only..." I frowned at him, pointing a finger accusingly. "You stole my boyfriend."

The god huffed.

"Now I'm sure Keith didn't mean much to you," I continued, pacing in front of the old man. "But he was a good guy, and he didn't

147

deserve what happened to him."

I turned him. "You played him. That's not a very Jehovah-y thing to do."

Jehovah crossed his arms over his bearded chest. "What are you trying to say to me, mortal?"

I watched him carefully. He was doing the intimidating thing, but I could sense an underlying uneasiness. I imitated his stance.

"I thought that it was weird, at first," I said. "You and Satan are enemies, on opposite sides. You oppose each other, like, always."

I rubbed my chin with one hand, propping the elbow on the other arm. Exaggeration was good for the bravado. "So, why, I asked myself, why would Satan try to stop me, those many months ago?" I threw my arms out to the side. "I mean, I had to be crazy to think that, right? He was subtle about it, don't get me wrong. But he was trying to get me to stop."

Jehovah shrugged his shoulders. "I don't really pay attention to that creature."

I snorted and began ticking off points on my fingers. "You put those Runespells into Keith's hands. You set Bob on his little quest. You had the great plan to kick off the end of the world. And I was tapped to stop you."

I began pacing again, trying to work off the nerves that kept squeezing my stomach and weakening my legs. "So why would Satan try to stop me, when I was trying to stop you?"

I paused. "I can only think of two reasons. One," I held up a finger. "You started this whole thing as some sort of convoluted plan to actually stop the end of the world by starting it."

I shrugged. "Problem is, you had everyone worried. If you were doing a suppression burn, so to speak, surely someone else would have been able to figure that out."

I turned to him and shot him a disdainful look, hoping he wasn't in a smiting mood. "You aren't exactly the god of smarts, you know."

I watched his face turn red with anger. His beard flickered for a moment, disappearing and reappearing quickly. I nodded. Confirmation.

I held up two fingers. "The second reason that I could think of is that you two are on the same side." I stopped pacing and held up my hands in an exaggerated shrug of confusion. "But how could that be? You have always been on opposing sides. In fact," I put my hand back to my chin, "it's kind of been a defining characteristic of your goodness and power, that you oppose Satan. Or that he opposes you. I mean, that polarity is the whole basis of many sects of Christianity. You know, the ones that claim you are either 'for God' or 'for Satan'?"

I put my hands on my hips and cocked my head. "No real options outside of that. And yet, by your own book, you created Satan."

I saw the god flinch at that. His appearance flickered again. I stood with my feet apart, ready to drive home my point. "Or maybe you didn't create Satan," I said in a low voice. "Maybe... you ARE Satan."

I knew he would be angry at my words, so I was braced for his burst of anger. It was still terrifying.

"You dare, mortal?" he shouted. "You insult my name? You question my power? You dare to suggest such an abomination?"

I held out my hands, palms up, to indicate the god in front of me, satisfaction battling terror in my gut. "I can see you!" I said. "Right now. You are... flickering from Jehovah to Satan. I can see you doing it!"

Jehovah began to grow, quickly doubling in size as he changed from one form to the other. "You should not have been able to know this!" he raged. "You cannot be allowed to know this!"

I cringed at his anger, trying not to cower too much. I felt a tendril of doubt creeping through my mind.

Then I remembered something Mercy had said, many months ago. The game is directed by humans. The gods can use them only to a degree.

The realization hit me, and I looked up at the god, intimidating as all get out, but... nothing else. I stood up straight and raised my chin. "What are you going to do about it?" I challenged him, swallowing my fear. "What can you do?"

The creature roared. "I will destroy you! I AM! I am all-powerful and I can destroy you in an instant!"

I shrugged. If he'd really been willing and able to snuff out my life, he would have done it by now with as angry as he was. "You might have the ability, but I don't think you have the capability."

Jehovah stopped. "You doubt me?"

I shook my head. "Not at all. It's just that, gods can't interfere with human choices. You could kill me – you have the power to do so. But it isn't within the realm of possibility that you can do it. You can't take away my knowledge and free will like that."

He stared at me for a long moment. Then he threw back his head and laughed. He shrunk back down to normal human size, taking on the guise of Satan as he did so.

"My clever, clever Nicola," he chuckled. "You certainly make things interesting for me, don't you?"

I shrugged. "I do my best."

Satan shook his head. "Well, I guess I'm just going to have to step up my game because of you."

He started to turn away, then he hesitated. "I may not be able to destroy you directly," he said in his smooth voice, "but I have other ways to remove problems."

"Yeah, yeah," I said, waving my hand in a circle, indicating he should get on with it. "Death, destruction, plummeting stock markets. I get it."

He glared at me with his gorgeous eyes. "I don't think you do." He smiled, but it wasn't a pleasant smile. "But you will."

• • •

I stood in the middle of the hallway, trying to figure out where else I should search for the strong box. I only had the rest of the day to find it before I had to put the key back or risk discovery.

I went over all the details that I knew about the Rod, about Nancy, about the Selection ceremony, but nothing was coming to me.

"Nicola?"

I turned at the voice. "Oh, hi, Kaitlyn," I said. I thought about commenting on her avoiding me, but I decided to let her take the lead.

"Are you... busy?" she asked. Her accent was stronger today than it had been before. She seemed very nervous, her dark eyes moving around as if trying to catch everything that moved. "I need to talk to you."

I followed her to her room and she gestured for me to sit on the bed. She paced the floor. I let my eyes go lax and looked at her energy. She was tense and nervous, but not about me. Maybe about whatever she wanted to say.

"Kaitlyn," I said softly. "You can tell me anything."

She stopped and blew her cheeks out. "I know," she admitted. "At least, I think so. But this is big."

I grinned at her. "Bigger than stealing magic pendants?" I asked.

She cocked her head to the side. "Maybe," she murmured. "Maybe they are the same thing."

I frowned, trying to make sense of what she was saying.

"Nicola," she said, taking my hands in hers. "I am also here, at the Center, under false pretenses."

I gaped at her. "What?"

She moved over to the dresser and pulled out a small black wallet. She flicked it open with a practiced move, showing a badge and ID. "I'm a federal agent," she said quietly. "I'm here under-cover. We heard some suspicious things about this place. I was sent to find out if it was true."

I nodded slowly. Everything I knew about Kaitlyn was beginning to make some sense. "And it is?"

"Yeah," she said. "And we are going to bust this place wide open." She looked at me. "Tomorrow."

I frowned. "That doesn't give me much time..." I began. "You will take the Rod and Zaro's pendant when you arrest them, won't you?"

Kaitlyn nodded. "It'll be taken as evidence. If you get what you need before the bust, though..." She shrugged. "What we don't find, we can't take."

I took a deep breath. "Thank you for the heads up," I said.

"That's not all," Kaitlyn continued. "I also need someone, at least one person, who will testify about Zaro raping them," she said.

I swallowed. Not many of the women would be likely to do that. I'd had such a hard time with the whole thing, and I knew about the energy effects. It would have to be me to step up and testify, and that meant reliving the whole thing over and over again.

I shook my head. If I did that, everyone would know. I'd have to deal with the shame, the guilt, the pity, and even the hate of those who would believe I was at fault. And it would be easy for them to think that. Energy and magic wasn't exactly the same thing as a drug, leaving a residue for forensics. But if I didn't, Zaro would get away with the rapes. I couldn't let that happen.

I looked up at Kaitlyn. Her eyes filled with compassion and understanding.

"I'll do it," I said, my voice cracking. "Take the bastard down, and I'll tell everyone what he did." Then, I grinned. "At least I don't have to worry about putting the key back."

CHAPT 25

I hustled Maria into the common room for lunch, just an hour before the Selection ceremony. According to Kaitlyn, the raid would start a few minutes before the Selection began. I sat the girl down on a seat near the far back corner, hoping she would be safest there.

"Maria," I said, looking into her face. "I want to get us out of here. Would you like to leave?"

She nodded.

"Good." I looked out over the crowd filling the room. "I have some things I need to do to make sure that happens. I want you to stay here. Eat your lunch, but stay in this area, okay?"

Maria clung to my arm. "You will come back?"

I smiled at her. "If I don't come back right away, do what Kaitlyn says. She'll make sure you stay safe until I can get back."

She frowned but nodded her agreement.

I felt bad leaving her. I just didn't know what else to do. This was my last chance to get the Runespells, especially since I wouldn't have to worry about getting caught. The raid would cover those tracks nicely. I wasn't really even sure exactly what I was going to do, I just knew I had to try.

As I climbed the staircase, I had the surprising thought of questioning Zaro about the Rod. I turned the thought over in my mind and shrugged to myself. Maybe he'd let something slip, but it was better than wandering around and hoping I didn't get caught by Nancy on the fourth floor.

I found Zaro on the third floor, talking to one of the women from the Mother's Garden. She was staring into his eyes, tears running down her face. Zaro seemed angry.

I waited until they were both looking the other way, then snuck in the bathroom doorway and peeked around the corner.

"You know the rules, Lorena," Zaro said impatiently. "You have a blessed child to look after. You must wait until the child is older to come back for my Touch." His gaze flickered down. "Much older."

He turned and walked away. The woman called after him, reaching out with one hand. After a moment, she bowed her head in defeat and turned towards me. She had an infant clutched in her other arm, though she didn't even glance at it.

I shivered, remembering the single-mindedness of being under the influence of Zaro's Touch. I hadn't realized he would restrict access to the Touch for the mothers of his children once they were no longer available for impregnation. I gritted my teeth, enraged at this new perspective of Zaro's abuse.

I waited until she passed by, then I scurried down the hallway to the end, where Zaro had disappeared into his room. It had been more than a week since I'd even wanted to be at this door again, and I fought a sudden wave of nausea combined with the molten heat of rage climbing my spine. It surprised me that the rage had returned. I hadn't felt it in weeks, and I'd nearly forgotten how strong it was. I struggled to push it back down.

The door started to open and I panicked, startled. I bolted down the hallway and ducked back into the bathroom. I leaned against the wall trying to catch my breath without making too much noise. As my fear subsided, I could hear Zaro talking to another man in the hallway.

"... get Nancy in a few minutes," he said. "Have her get the Rod from my room and bring it to me. We only have about half an hour before the Selection begins, so don't let her put you off..."

I pushed down the thrill of victory that ran through me, biting my tongue to keep from shouting. Zaro's voice trailed off as they moved into the stairwell. I peeked out the door and saw them taking the stairs. Zaro went down, and the other man went up.

I bit my lip and took a deep breath. Now or never, hero-girl.

I raced down the hallway and grabbed the doorknob to Zaro's room. For a moment, I was afraid it would be locked, but it turned easily in my hand. I entered the room, pushing down the memories of what had happened here.

I searched quickly, looking in the dresser and behind the thick floor-length curtains. Then, I got down and checked under the large bed.

Bingo.

I pulled the metal strong box out from under the bed frame and smirked. It was the same box that I'd gotten the key from in my vision. I pulled the chain out from under my tunic and willed the key off of it. It fell into my hand and I fumbled it into the lock. It finally clicked open and I lifted the lid.

I let out a breath I hadn't realized I was holding. The Rod lay in the bottom of the box, its shimmering ivory shaft gleaming in the dim light. I pulled it out and looked at the spot at the top of the shaft, just beneath the crystal at the tip.

There it was, a small silver bindrune embedded in the top of the shaft.

I tried to grab it, but I couldn't get my fingers in underneath the crystal. So I tried prying the crystal out of its setting, but it was too firmly mounted. I even stuck the Rod against the floor several times, trying to knock something loose.

Nothing.

I sighed and looked around, wondering what else to do. If I didn't get it out soon, I'd get caught with the Rod in my hand and the key off the chain.

The chain. The chain had bound the other Runespells, though they had been loose in my hand. I wondered if it would be able to pull the pendant out of the Rod.

I shrugged and pulled the chain out as far as it would go. I shoved part of it under the crystal, as close to the bindrune as I could get it. Then I willed the chain to catch the Runespell. The chain seemed to melt in the one spot touching the pendant, and I smiled as the Runespell attached to the chain. I tugged at the chain.

It was stuck.

I pulled harder, trusting that the magickal necklace wouldn't break. With a sudden ping, the chain released from the Rod.

I checked it, quickly, afraid I'd lost the Runespell. It was still there. Without thinking, I ran a finger over the newest pendant. Time froze, and the breath stopped in my throat. I heard a familiar chanting voice, deep and powerful, singing the words into being. I knew now that the voice was Odin's.

The voice repeated the opening verse over and over. "Learn to carve them, learn to read them, learn to stain them, learn to validate them, learn to summon them, learn to modify them, learn to share them, learn to use them."

I felt my pulse beating in time to the rhythm of the words of the Hávamál as they changed to another verse.

"I have learned the second spell: If any healing can be done to mankind, by magic, medicine, or technique; if any illness or injury can be healed by the same, then it shall be known, and it can be done, by the wielder of the spell."

I gasped as time unfroze and I shook my head. This Runespell was powerful, and it was a shame it had been so misused.

I glanced over the Rod and found that the bottom tip of the fake crystal had snapped off at an odd angle. Oh, well. I figured that by the time anyone noticed the imperfection, shit would already be hitting the fan, if everything went according to plan.

I stuck the Rod back into the box, shut the lid and turned the key. I left the key in the box's lock and shoved the whole thing back under the bed. I stood up to leave and froze. There were voices outside the door. One of them was the distinct, cold sound of Nancy's voice.

I glanced around the room, searching for a hiding place. My gaze fell on the ostentatious curtains. I bounded across the room and flattened myself against the wall, letting one of the curtains fall around me, hopefully hiding me from view. I focused on controlling my breathing, keeping it steady and quiet, as the door opened.

"It's under the bed," Nancy said. "Pull it out."

I heard the clinking of metal on metal over the sound of the box sliding across the floor.

"The key. It's gone."

A male voice chimed in. "There's already a key in the lock. Maybe you left it there last time?"

"Doubtful," Nancy snapped. "I never take it off the keychain. Well, open it up."

There was a metallic clink and a thud.

"Give it to me," Nancy ordered. There was a long pause. "Give this to Zaro. Show him this."

"It's broke!' the man said.

"Obviously," Nancy said. "Tell him to meet me here. I have to check on... something."

I heard the door open and close. Before I could move, the sound of the box sliding along the floor had me catching my breath. It was followed by the sound of dresser drawers opening and closing.

Nancy was still in the room. And she was looking for something.

I began to fear that she was just going to wait in the room for Zaro. Then I heard her mutter softly to herself, and the door opened and closed again.

I leaned against the wall, feeling weak from the adrenaline leaving my system. I gasped a few breaths before I felt able to move again. I untangled myself from the curtains and made my way across the room, stepping over the strong box that was pushed only partway under the bed.

I reached for the door just as it burst open. I stared at Zaro's enraged face as his body filled the opening.

CHAPT 26

I gasped and turned to run. I felt the weight of Zaro's body hit my back, knocking the wind out of me. I fell onto the bed, gasping for air under his weight.

I could hear him screaming in my ear and I struggled to get up. I felt a hand on the back of my neck, and my face was pushed deep into the bed covers. The thick blankets covered my nose and mouth, and I couldn't take in a breath. I kicked and flailed my arms, trying to dislodge his bulk and lift my head.

Suddenly, I felt the warmth of a soft blanket in the chill of winter, and my arms fell to the bed. I gasped in the bed covers as the relaxation of Zaro's touch filled me.

He was Touching me. Again.

My head cleared at the angry thought. I could feel the molten heat creeping up my spine once again. I thought, for a moment, that I should let it take me over. But I had to make sure I got the Runespell. I had to make sure Maria was safe. I couldn't risk whatever the anger had in store for me. So, I pushed it back down, holding it at bay.

A loud pop rang out in the room, and the pressure on my neck lessened enough for me to take in several gulps of air.

"Lazaro Gaona, you are under arrest for sexual assault, rape as an accomplice, coercion, fraud, conspiracy to commit fraud, tax evasion, racketeering, and false advertising."

I choked when I heard the last charge. It seemed almost ridiculous in light of the horrible acts Zaro had committed.

"Step away from the woman, Zaro," the familiar voice continued. "Or we will be adding attempted murder to the charges."

Zaro's weight suddenly lifted from my body. I pushed myself up and glanced around. Zaro had retreated to the far side of the room, behind the bed.

Kaitlyn, gun drawn, ID out, but still in her cream linen, was rounding the bed. She glanced down at me, her eyes flashing. Except for her hair being in the Bantu knots she favored, she looked just like the creature from my vision.

"You okay, Nicola?" she asked.

"Yemaya," I whispered.

She shot me a confused look, so I nodded that I was okay. She turned her full attention back to Zaro. The man held his hands out at his sides. He stood still, patient and slightly smiling. I immediately knew something was wrong.

Kaitlyn put her ID away and pulled a pair of handcuffs out of her pocket. She walked towards Zaro, reaching the hand with the cuffs towards his wrist. I saw his hand turn towards hers, reaching out to meet her touch. I froze, knowing that his Touch would give Kaitlyn the Peace, and she would be too entranced to fight him.

"No!" I screamed in warning to her, and her head whipped around at the sound.

Her eyes met mine a split second before Zaro's hand fell on her skin. Her dark eyes glazed and her shoulders relaxed. I choked back a sob as I watched my friend slip under at the power of the Touch.

I glanced at the door as the other agents entered. They entered in formation, blocking the escape and holding weapons ready to fire, true to their extensive training. But their training didn't cover this.

I looked back at Kaitlyn, my mind racing with the boost of fear. Kaitlyn, a federal agent who had gone deep undercover to expose the abuses brought on the people of the Healing Center by their leader, Zaro. And now he held her captive as surely as if he'd held a knife to her throat.

"Agent Jardine," one of the feds called out. "Status?"

Kaitlyn blinked and turned her head toward the man's voice. Zaro shot the man a patronizing smile.

"Too late," he drawled. "Stand back."

Without the power of Zaro's Touch, Kaitlyn would likely have been able to draw on her training, disabling the man quickly. Moving without having to think about it. That is what the extensive training was for, after all, to overcome human errors brought on by emotional reactions and poor judgment.

I gasped, realization hitting me.

"Kaitlyn!" I called out, pitching my voice low and projecting loudly across the room. "Agent! Take down the suspect!"

Kaitlyn blinked slowly, a slight frown crossing her face.

I stepped forward and cried out again. "I'm talking to you, Agent Jardine! Secure this room! Now!"

Kaitlyn moved, slowly at first, but with sure motions. Her arm swept up in front her her, pushing Zaro's hand away from her arm and gripping his wrist in her hand. I saw Zaro move his free hand towards the pendant around his throat.

"Kaitlyn!" I cried. "Agent Jardine! Secure the pendant!"

The dark woman moved like a flash, blocking Zaro's hands and grabbing the pendant, yanking the chain off his neck. She pivoted and tossed it to me without an instant of hesitation.

I caught the pendant in the air and gasped as time stopped. I heard the familiar chanting voice, singing the words over and over. "Learn to carve them, learn to read them..."

I felt my pulse beating out the rhythm of the words as they changed to the next verse.

"I have learned the first spell: A song within the heart, a nobility that is not royal, a divinity among mortals. It is named help, aid, and comfort, for that is what it brings to those who need it; the touch of peace and pleasure to those in pain."

Each word burned into my memory, and I understood how to use the Runespell. I knew what it could do, and what I was capable of with it in my hands. And I understood just how much Zaro had bastardized the power.

Time returned to normal and my breath released. I stared at the pendant for a moment, then I pulled the chain around my neck from beneath my shirt. I touched the pendant to the silver necklace. The metal strands of the wrapping around the Runespell parted, and the sigil held inside bound itself to the necklace, joining the others.

I looked up to find Kaitlyn being helped to her feet by her fellow agents. But Zaro was gone.

"What happened?" I asked.

One of the men nearby eyed me. "The suspect slipped out a hidden door." He nodded towards the back wall, and I could see a section of the wood paneling was ajar. "He made it to the stairwell before we got to this door. But all of the exits are covered, so..." He shrugged.

I caught Kaitlyn's eye. "What about Nancy?"

Kaitlyn shook her head. "I don't know."

I ran out the door. Kaitlyn protested, but she followed me down the hall and up the stairs.

I got to the fourth floor and found Nancy in the corner room with two agents watching her. She wrote in the patient chart before she placed her hands behind her back for the waiting agents. She looked up when I rushed into the room, and I thought I saw a flash of a sneer on her impassive face.

"He's not here," Nancy said in her cold, emotionless voice. "Zaro. He had an exit built into the basement."

I saw her glance towards the patient, and I felt my own lip curl.

"Stealing from us will cost you more than you ever thought," she continued.

Kaitlyn grabbed the front of Nancy's white shirt. "Do you know where Zaro's going?"

The nurse ignored Kaitlyn's manhandling. "He's going after the girl," she said, staring at me. "And her grandmother. Like a wolf in the woods, it seems."

I frowned. Bob started laughing, a deep, malicious cackle. Nancy glanced at Bob again, a smirk crossing her face.

I shook my head and raced down the stairs. The common room was filled with people looking confused, agents looking for injured, women weeping that the agents were wrong.

I pushed through the crowd to the back corner of the room. Maria looked up when I approached, and I swept her up into a hug.

"You're okay?" I asked.

"Yeah," Maria said. "I stayed right where you told me to." She looked up at me with a hopeful smile. "Do we get to go home now?"

I smiled at her, certain that if things didn't work out with her mother, Maria would be perfectly happy coming with me. She would probably spend hours playing with Ella in the woods.

I gasped.

The woods. My home. Nancy had said the girl and her

grandmother. She had to mean Ella and my mother. She had said a wolf in the woods. Then Bob had laughed.

Bob, who had witnessed Keith's will. The will that left everything to our daughter, Ella. He knew where she lived. And she was with my mother, her grandmother, in a small town in a national forest.

CHAPT 27

I got to the airport in record time, thanks to Kaitlyn using one of the classic unmarked black SUVs with the lights and sirens. I checked departure times and found the terminal for the flight leaving for Louisville first, since it was actually closer to my home than Indy was. They had an extra seat available, and I paid for it, thankful that Kaitlyn had talked me into grabbing my personal items, including my purse with my credit cards.

I paused before turning from the counter, and I asked the woman if she'd seen a man with Zaro's description. She shook her head. I sighed, relieved, then looked over at the other two terminal counters.

One was empty, but I walked over to the other, Kaitlyn at my heels. I explained to the man at the counter that I was trying to find out if I'd missed "my friend" and gave him the description.

He frowned. "I did see a guy like that," he said. "He stuck out because of the weird clothes." He glanced at my outfit. "Like yours. All tan and loose."

I swallowed. "Did he purchase a flight?"

"No," the man shook his head. "He was booking a chartered flight." He clicked his tongue. "They are pretty expensive. I was pretty shocked when he paid in cash." The man caught my questioning look and shrugged. "It was slow. I people watch."

I thanked him and we rushed over to the chartering counter. The man behind the counter glanced at Kaitlyn, dismissing her. Then he looked me up and down and grinned.

"What can I do for you, pretty lady," he drawled.

I rolled my eyes and gave him Zaro's description. "Have you seen him? Did he book a flight with you?"

The man frowned. "I don't usually talk about my customers..."

I sighed.

Kaitlyn stepped forward and flashed her ID. "That man threatened her kid, and he's escaped federal custody. We need to know if he got on a plane here."

The man went pale. "Hey, I didn't know he was a crook," he stuttered. "I swear!" He fumbled with some paperwork and handed Kaitlyn a flight plan. "That's him, right there."

Kaitlyn scanned the document and turned to me. "He left fifteen minutes ago. And it's a direct flight to Indianapolis." She sighed. "He'll beat you by at least an hour, even with you going in through Louisville."

"Oh, gods," I moaned. "What can we do?"

The woman pulled out her phone. "You get home as soon as possible. I'll get things cleared up to send the local feds after him." She pressed her lips together. "I hate bureaucracy. They may not make it before you do. They'll be coming from Indianapolis. But I'll try."

I nodded and glanced at the clock. "I better get ready to go. Boarding is in twenty minutes." I touched her arm. "And make sure Maria is okay for me?"

She nodded, and I turned towards the security checkpoint. "Good luck, Nicola," she called.

• • •

During the flight, I dozed off, exhausted from the constant adrenaline, lulled by the steady buzz of the engines, and frustrated by my inability to do anything to change the speed of the plane. I dreamed of my first meeting with Huginn and Muninn. The ravens had come to me in the astral plane, offering me the information I'd needed – in the form of a tiny pearl.

Muninn had jabbed it into my throat, giving me the memories of thousands of sensations, scents, tastes, emotions. There had been so much information that it had literally crashed my mind. I'd had to spend hours in meditation, reviewing the memories, before I'd been able to use them to find the four Runespells that Keith had been given.

I dreamed of Muninn jumping on my chest, jabbing the tiny sphere into my open mouth. I felt my body reacting to the memories, jerking and twitching. But this time, I was an objective observer, present in my body, but not directly experiencing what I'd gone through.

I felt my mind crashing, and Muninn cried out. I remembered hearing the croaking voice before, though I hadn't been able to make out the words. Now, in this dream, they were crystal clear.

"Rage your power!"

I jerked awake, jostling the woman next to me. I ignored her glare and checked the time. We would be landing soon.

•   •   •

I raced down the roads from the busy streets of Indie to the country highways near my mother's house. I pushed the rental car past the speed limit as much as I dared, gritting my teeth at every slow car or stop light I encountered.

I finally got to her apartment and raced to the door. I pounded on it, peering into the window to one side. There were no lights, no movement, nothing. I cried out my frustration and anger. Where would they be?

Zaro was going off of information that Bob had gotten from Keith and the will. Keith knew about my mother and where she lived. But the will had had my address on it.

I raced back to the car, cursing my limp loudly. I only noticed that it was getting dark out when the automatic lights turned on when I started the car. I turned down the familiar streets, heading for my home about a mile out of town. I turned down the dirt road that ran past my house and gunned the engine. I just hoped I wouldn't be pulled over by some overzealous cop looking to hand out some extra tickets.

Gravel sprayed when I hit my driveway at around forty miles an hour, and I braked hard to stop. I jumped out of the car and raced to the door. I gasped. The door was hanging ajar.

I briefly considered the subtle approach, but Zaro had to know I was coming, and I had nothing I could use to ambush him. This was going to be a head to head confrontation.

I pushed open the door, letting it bang against the wall, and yelled at the top of my lungs. "Zaro! Where are you, you little piss-ant?"

I listened in the dark for any sign of my family or the man who had threatened them. There was a small shuffling noise from the patio. I headed in that direction, keeping my senses alert. I saw him through the doors, holding my daughter by the throat and my mother by her hair.

My mother looked exhausted and Ella had dried tears streaking her cheeks. The hand at Ella's neck held a knife. I snarled. It was one of my really good, expensive kitchen knives. I threw open the patio doors and stepped outside.

"Let them go, Zaro," I growled. "Pretend to be a man for once. Stop hiding behind my family and face me."

"Why would I do that?" He asked, stroking Ella's cheek with his thumb. "I rather like these two."

I realized in a flash that my best option would be to disarm him with words. I remembered how that had ended almost a year ago, when I faced down Rowan in a gas station. My step-sister had lost it and had trashed the store, and her "normal" future along with it. But I had managed to win the battle of wits and energy, and the rest had been more about the circumstances than the battle.

I gathered my chaotic energy and laughed, a harsh and derogatory chuckle. "I knew you were a fucking coward," I spat out. "If you thought you could beat me, you'd know you could hunt them down once I'm taken care of." I sneered at him. "But you know you can't beat me, don't you?"

Zaro sneered. "You have no idea what I can do! I have the power of God behind me!"

I leaned my weight on one hip. "Oh, you mean Jehovah?" I grinned, maliciously. "That schmuck of a deity couldn't even stop me when I was right there insulting him to his damn face. You think he's gonna help your pathetic ass?"

The man stepped forward, angrily, releasing my mother's hair and shoving past her. She staggered and fell to her hands and knees. "You lie!" Zaro snarled.

I caught my mother's eye. "Call the police. Go!"

She stood and ran around the house, looking back several times. I breathed a small sigh of relief that at least one of Zaro's hostages was free. I turned back to the man. He still held my daughter. He wouldn't get away with that. The boiling heat of my anger began to rise, but I held it down.

"I can't tell if you were smart, doing at least part of what I told you," I said, lifting one hand, then the other. "Or stupid for reacting to such an obvious insult." I smirked. "I bet Nancy wouldn't think too highly of you right now."

Zaro laughed. "That frigid bitch never thought anything of me. She was too busy with her obsession with curing the world, at all costs, to ever have any feelings for me or anyone else."

I shrugged, pushing at the hot pressure of rage in my neck. "I dunno," I drawled. "She seemed awfully emotional towards Bob, last I saw."

Zaro's face twisted in a furious snarl. "You lie!" he said again.

"Nope." I rocked on my heels. "She seemed quite cozy with her precious patient." I looked the man up and down. "Plus, the cost of Nancy's healing seems irrelevant, since you managed to pass it on to the customer, all nice and tidy."

"What?" Zaro shot me a look of pure confusion.

I paused. Maybe he hadn't been in on Nancy's Healing scam. "You didn't know she was Healing for cash on the side?" I shook my head at the man. "From what I saw, it was a pretty penny, too."

Zaro snarled. "She wouldn't do that - "

"What?" I snapped. "Disrespect you? Keep you out of the loop? Ha! No wonder you had to force women to be with you. Even your own wife would rather share thousands of dollars with another man, a man covered in fucking burns, than be with you!"

Zaro roared and sliced across Ella's neck with the knife. He pushed my daughter aside as he rushed towards me, knife raised to attack.

I saw the red liquid spurt from my baby girl's throat, and time stood still. I watched the terror and shock on her face as she fell into the dirt. The red lava in my neck pushed past whatever resistance I had left for it, and rushed over my ears to the top of my skull, filling my head with a hot numbness.

I panicked.

I remembered the last time I'd felt the rage, one of only two times in my life that I'd let it loose, uncontrolled. I'd been locked in a basement room with Mercy and Joseph, and I'd negotiated with Bob. Joseph and Mercy had turned on me, their fears temporarily overcoming our friendship. They'd accused me of making things worse and demanded to know what to do.

But I hadn't known what to do. So I lost it. I lost control and I lost my humanity for – I don't even know how long. I'd managed to focus my rage, not on my friends, but on the wall behind me. And I'd beaten at the wall with my arms, feet, and even my head, until my body was too weak and injured to continue.

Afterward, Joseph and Mercy had taken care of me, but I'd seen the wariness in Joseph's eyes. It hadn't lasted long, but it had been there. Mercy, though, had looked at me as though I'd given her some puzzle to solve. I'd suspected that she had known something more about what had happened, but I hadn't had the chance to ask her about it.

I feared my anger and the violence that came with it. I didn't know what else to do about it. Then, I remembered the dream I'd had on the plane. Muninn's words, that he had called out before I'd passed out those many months before, had been finally clear.

Rage your power.

But that wasn't quite right. He'd said those words, in that order, but there was a slight pause in the middle. He'd said, *Rage, your power.*

I raised my eyes to Zaro's face, twisted with his own anger. I glanced at Ella, crying in the dirt. I thought about my mother, running for help in the middle of the night. Clarity filled my mind, overlapping the heat.

If rage was my power, I thought, it might just be time to embrace it.

I let myself feel the anger. I let it fill me, my acceptance of it changing the slow, heavy red lava into the white-hot light of a super-nova. I felt angrier than I'd ever felt before, and it was power.

CHAPT 28

The rage climbed into my head, filling my sight with red that cleared into... something else. I could see everything so clearly. Shapes stood out sharply in the dim light, like night vision goggles, only red instead of green.

My face felt numb, and my skin felt full, swollen, like the way my mouth felt after a trip to the dentist. All of my senses seemed muted until I focused on Zaro.

I could see the pulse beating in Zaro's throat. It called to me. I could smell his fear, and it was like perfume. I could hear the gasping of his breath, a song to my ears. I could feel the warmth of his body in the cool night air, like a flame that drew me to him.

In my mind, I smiled, indulging in the power that rushed through my body like flood waters from a broken dam. Physically, I screamed my power and anger as I rushed to meet Zaro's attack.

The Eleventh Runespell burned against my chest, drawing the smallest part of my attention, and I let the battle-pendant guide my movements as I'd done so long ago, facing down Bob. I swung my arm around at Zaro's throat, striking the blow with my forearm a split second before our bodies crashed together. He gagged and staggered. I used his stumble to land another blow with my fist to the side of his face. He shoved at my chest with both hands and we broke apart.

I lashed out with a fist and grazed his scalp when he dodged it. He landed a blow to my shoulder that threw me back a step. I recovered and stepped forward twice, thrusting my fists in tight jabs at his face, chest and neck. He took two of the blows on his chin, his head snapping back each time.

I pressed forward, ignoring the guidance of the pendant and the blow that Zaro landed in the center of my stomach. In the back of my mind, I could feel the wave of nausea as my gut absorbed the impact, but the white-hot numbness of my rage kept it dull and distant. I managed to hit him full in the mouth, and I grinned at the sight of blood welling up around his lips. Still swinging my fists in tight circles in front of me, I hit him again and again, in the face, in the chest.

He ducked his head and covered it with his arms, but I was too enraged to care. I grabbed one of his wrists with both hands and bent it back sharply, pleasure shooting through me when I felt the snap of bone under my fingers. I vaguely heard the man's howl of pain as I dealt a backhanded blow across his face with my left fist, quickly followed by a jab to his ear with my right.

I pressed my advantage and lashed out with my fists over and over. Memories flashed through my mind – Zaro Touching my arm, Zaro holding a knife to Ella's throat, Zaro thrusting into my body, Zaro hurting the women at the Center, Zaro cutting into Ella's neck, Zaro helping not-so-good ol' Bob, Zaro making mothers forget their children, Zaro hunting my family, Zaro attacking me...

The memories and the rhythmic blows filled my mind, and I blanked out everything else around me. There was only muted darkness with muffled sounds and a tight circle of awareness around my fists landing on his upper body.

Then he was laying on the ground as I straddled him. I howled with rage as I smashed my fists into the body lying beneath me. I felt bones give and flesh squish under my onslaught. But I couldn't stop hitting him. I had lost the ability to control my own body. And I had lost the ability to care.

But when he didn't move or respond, my rage began to fade, and the blows slowed. My eyes ached from tears that barely managed to squeeze from my burning eyes. I collapsed onto my hands and knees, half sprawled over the unmoving body beneath me.

A cool hand brushed over my forehead, and I looked up into Mercy's ice blue eyes.

"It's done," she said.

I dropped my head and looked down at Zaro. His blood-covered face was misshapen, nose flattened but swollen, puffy eyes closed with bruising and cuts. For a moment, I was horrified at what I'd done, convinced I'd killed him. But he took a gurgling breath.

Then I remembered the reason I'd gone into the rage in the first place. The image of Ella's blood crashed into my mind, driving me to my feet.

"Ella!" Mercy's hands steadied me on my feet. My limbs were weak, and I felt disoriented and a little queasy. The Valkyrie helped me limp over to where my daughter sat in the dirt, one hand pressed against her throat.

I moved her hand from her neck and examined the cut. It wasn't deep and, though there was quite a bit of blood, it wasn't pumping like an arterial bleed would.

I enfolded Ella in my arms and murmured, over and over, "My baby, my baby."

"Nicola," Mercy said. "You have the healing Runespell."

I reached for Ella's throat, then froze. My brain, slowly starting up again, was analyzing the situation, the consequences. I heard sirens approaching in the distance and I shook my head. "I... I can't," I said.

Mercy gave me a confused look.

"If I tell them what happened, but Ella isn't injured, they won't believe it was self-defense," I explained. "I would likely go to prison and they would take her away."

Mercy frowned, but nodded. "At least she's not seriously hurt."

Ella looked up at me. "Mama?" she whimpered. "What happened to you?"

I looked up at Mercy, then buried my face in Ella's dark hair. "I'm not really sure, honey," I said. "But I'll figure it out."

"You embraced your rage," Mercy said as if that explained everything. She must have noticed the look on my face. "Since the... situation in Bob's basement, I've suspected you were a Berserker," she explained.

I frowned. "Crazy naked man with an axe?"

Mercy laughed. "Not quite." She squatted down to talk. "More like a person who, when they embrace their anger, they channel the spirit of an animal in battle." She shrugged. "Most of the time it's a bear, but you didn't fight like you were channeling a bear. You were more like a large cat."

I frowned. "So, what does that mean?"

"Now that you've embraced it, instead of it just pushing through, you'll be able to learn to control it. To use it." She smiled at me. "To explore the gifts it gives."

"Gifts?"

Mercy nodded. "You can take on certain characteristics of the animal. With bears, it tends to be immense strength. With you?" She grinned. "Well, we never know what you are gonna do, do we?"

My head turned as the sound of the sirens slowed and stopped around where my driveway was. "They're here," I murmured.

Mercy stood and looked through the patio doors to the front door. She nodded. "And that's my cue to leave." She turned back to look at me. "You did such a good job."

I snorted. "You could have helped more with..." I gestured to Zaro's body, feeling bitter.

"No," Mercy said. "I couldn't."

"Bullshit!" I said. "I've seen you fight! You could have taken him out."

Mercy stared at me for a moment. "Have you ever seen me fight a human?"

I opened my mouth to retort, then paused. I thought about it. "I... I guess not."

Mercy sighed. "I've told you. As a god creature, I cannot interfere with human choices. As horrible a person as Zaro was, he was still a person. I could not do anything." She shot me a compassionate look. "I could only try to help and encourage you. And only because you asked me to."

I frowned but I nodded. It was a crap situation, but I realized those rules that prevented Mercy from fighting my battles were the same rules that had kept Jehovah-Satan from squishing me like a bug when I confronted him with all the sarcasm I could muster.

The Valkyrie turned away and jogged into the woods, out of sight. She had no more than reached the trees when police officers in black shirts came around the corner of the house. Other people in navy blue EMT jackets clustered behind them.

I called out for help and several of them rushed over.

CHAPT 29

It took several hours to explain what happened, going over the scene at my home again and again. My mother told the officers that Zaro had shown up at my house while she was getting Ella settled for bed. They'd been staying where Ella was more comfortable, since I'd been gone so long.

Zaro had pushed his way into the house and held them at knifepoint in the living room until my headlights had announced my arrival. Then, he'd dragged her and Ella into the back yard to wait for me.

I, meanwhile, told them several times that I just wasn't sure what had happened after my mother left. I told them that Zaro had gotten angry, and that I'd seen him cut Ella across the throat. I figured they could piece together what I'd done to Zaro, but I wasn't sure how I would react to retelling the story.

They didn't seem very happy with my lack of detail, but Kaitlyn swept in with her federal ID badge and words like "jurisdiction" and "interdepartmental cooperation." When one of the small-town cops cracked a racial joke, Kaitlyn walked up to him and told him off.

Then she turned around. "Anyone else want to make this about my beautiful black skin, instead of the terrorist organization we are tryin' to take down?"

At the word "terrorist," the locals got wide-eyed and backed off. There were murmurs about "not enough manpower" and "that's not in our budget." Finally, they left Kaitlyn and me alone in the tiny interrogation room of the local sheriff's office.

"How are you holdin' up?" she asked me, sitting across from me with an expression of genuine concern.

I shrugged. "All good, considering. When can I see Ella?"

Kaitlyn nodded. "I promise I'll be quick," she assured me. "Just go over this and make sure your contact info is right and the statement you gave these guys was transcribed correctly."

I scanned the document quickly, but completely. "Yeah, it's good."

She reached across the table and placed her hand over mine. "I'm really sorry about everything you went through," she said. "But I can't say I'm too upset about how it ended."

Kaitlyn stood up. "I'll be in touch about your testimony, and I'd recommend you get yourself into a therapist's office." She smiled. "Don't try to be brave. You're gonna need someone to talk to."

I nodded. "Thanks, Kaitlyn... er, Agent Jardine."

She grinned at me. "Honey, you can call me whatever you want. You cleaned up my case real nice."

I laughed, then I thought of the other little girl in my life. "How's Maria?"

Kaitlyn sighed. "The women are going to be treated for 'Stockholm's,'" she said, using air quotes. "They and their children will be placed by CPS after until everyone is back to... well, as close to normal as they can get."

"So, Maria will be in... what? Foster care?" I frowned. "Could she come stay with me?"

"Actually, that would be easiest," she admitted. "The papers Maria's mother signed at the Center do give you legal custody and, unlike many of the other guardians, you aren't suspected of... ulterior motives."

I nodded. "I think she and Ella will get along just fine," I said. "What happened to Bob? The patient in the corner room."

Kaitlyn frowned. "I don't know. Was he part of this whole thing, too?"

I shook my head. "I... I'm not sure. He's connected to the Runespells, but I don't know about the Center."

"I'll try and find out for you," Kaitlyn assured me. "Go see your daughter."

• • •

I let my mother drive me to the hospital to check on Ella. I was in no condition to be behind the wheel. We got to her room, where she was sitting up, eating ice cream and watching some cartoon with talking animals.

I breathed a sigh of relief and sat on her bed where I could hold her. She let me squeeze her for a few minutes, then wriggled free to get another bite of frozen chocolate. Ella was excited to hear about Maria coming to stay with us, and I spent several hours catching my mother up on what had happened. By the time we ran out of things to talk about, Ella had fallen asleep.

The next morning, I was able to take her home, with my mother coming to stay for a few days. I wasn't sure if she was coming to help with Ella or to keep an eye on me. I couldn't blame her either way.

● ● ● ●

It only took a day of being home before the Norns returned. I knew when they appeared because the skin on the back of my neck started crawling, even before I turned to face them.

"You did well," they said in their creepy synchronized voices.

I shrugged off the creepy feeling. The Norns, being the keepers of destiny, weren't necessarily bound by the same rules as other god-creatures. They could interfere with human choices. But I doubted they could do more to me than I'd already been through. Or that was still coming with the inevitable future quests I was going to face.

"Now what do you want?" I asked, wearily.

The three women exchanged glances. "The Runespells - "

"Are mine to use," I interrupted.

They stared at me with their cold eyes, not quite seeing me, but looking at something around where I was. "What will you do with the Healing sigil?" they asked.

I thought about it. "I... I don't know," I admitted.

"Will you travel the world Healing those in need? Will you leave your child to help others?" They moved forward, closing in around me. "Or will you deny the sick the power at your command?"

I frowned. That choice wasn't something I had considered, but I knew they were right. I wouldn't be able to stop helping people if I had the power to do something.

"Will you anger Hel the same way that Nancy did?" they hissed. "Will you threaten the Weaving for your own righteousness?"

I cowered under their collective gaze. "I... I don't... "

"What will you do, mortal, with the power of Healing? What choices, what sacrifices will you make to save your fellow humans? Will you deny death itself? Will you deny the gods their due?" They came so close, their clothing brushed against my skin, like snakes slithering over me.

I dropped my head, hiding my face in my hands. I could see the situation unfolding, a long line of hard choices that would be just as horrible as the Selection had been. "What else can I do? Isn't that what the spell is for?"

I felt them back away, the pressure of their closeness easing. I looked up at them. They were watching me.

"Once in a generation, there is born a mortal with the power to see the Weaving. They can use the Second Runespell without undoing the Threads. They can make those choices. That is their destiny."

I grasped the pendants on the chain around my neck. "A mortal? And he, or she, can... deal with that... that dilemma?"

"That is their destiny," the Norns repeated.

The anxiety that had begun to fill me when I realized what keeping the Healing sigil would mean for me lifted. There was someone out there who was built to handle this, someone who could take the burden of the constant choices out of my already full hands.

I stood up with as much dignity as I could manage. "Will you give this person the Runespell for me?" I asked.

The three women, in perfect synchronization, bowed slightly in my direction. "It is our duty to do so."

I removed the sigil from the chain, hesitating only a brief moment before I handed it to the robotic-looking Norn. I turned my head away as she took it, cold fingers sending a tremor through me. When I looked back, they were gone.

I sighed in relief.

CHAPT 30

Joseph came out to see me as soon as he found out I was back. We sat on the patio with our drinks, and I told him the entire story. Every horrid detail, including the call from Kaitlyn telling me Bob was nowhere to be found. Again.

I made it through until the end before I broke down crying. He let me sob until I was drained of the pain, the fear, the shame.

"Shit."

I rolled my swollen red eyes. "You've got such a way with words," I mumbled.

He shrugged. "It's a gift." He leaned forward. "But what did you expect? I'd beat that man senseless, but you took care of that."

I snorted.

"And it sounds like you did a pretty good job of it, too," Joseph finished, leaning back and raising his glass in my direction. "Don't you dare feel bad about any part of what you did. Most people would have done the same."

I rolled my shoulders.

He paused. "No, that's not right. Most people would have curled up in a ball and begged for mercy." He shook his head. "Not you, though."

I gave him a dirty look.

Joseph shot me a wicked grin. "Can't say if it's 'cause you're smarter than the average bear or 'cause you're just too damn stubborn to know any better."

I scowled at him. "Did you come all the way out here just to insult my intelligence?"

"Nope," he said, throwing back the rest of his wine. "I came all the way out here to sing karaoke."

• • •

Joseph dragged me to the local country karaoke bar, complete with a mechanical bull in the corner. I grumbled the whole way, half wishing that I could just stay home, curled up on my bed and feeling sorry for myself.

He insisted on choosing my first song on the karaoke stage. Against my half-hearted protests, he left to put in the request. I stayed, slumped in my chair, stirring the ice cubes in my empty drink with one of those tiny straw stirrers.

A glass plunked down in front of me. I blinked at the drink, and my eyes followed the arm up to a clean-cut face that stared down at me with hard eyes. He was dressed much like the rest of the guys in the bar: button-down shirt, blue jeans and cowboy boots.

I didn't recognize the man, and I opened my mouth to refuse the drink.

"The Wanderer said you would like Jack and Coke," he said in a quiet, rumbling voice that managed to carry over the noise of the bar.

I froze. The Wanderer. Odin?

The man gestured to the glass with the hand he'd used to set it down, holding his other arm close to his body. I noticed his hand was missing, not in the cleanly rounded stump that was more common in amputations, but in a mess of jagged skin.

I jerked my eyes back up to his face as he spoke again.

"I wanted to extend to you my respects for what you did," he said. He lifted his arm to indicate his missing hand. "Your sacrifice may not be as obvious as a hand or an eye, but it is as great, and as honorable."

I wiggled the remaining toes in my right shoe. The missing digits took some getting used to, but it was more an emotional loss now. I remembered the experiences, the death and violations, every time I put on my socks.

I looked back up at the man. He held my gaze for a long moment before giving a single, sharp nod. Then, he turned on his heel and left. Joseph appeared at the table, looking at the man walking away.

"Who was that?" he asked.

I swallowed the lump in my throat. "Tyr."

178

Joseph's eyebrows climbed up his forehead. "The Norse god of justice?"

I nodded. "He bought me a drink. He said it was for his respect for what I did."

Joseph peered into the crowd, though the man had disappeared. Then he shrugged. "Well, it makes sense. You exacted justice when you put that worthless piece of crap in a coma."

I shot him a questioning look.

"From what you've told me, Norse laws weren't known for pussy-footing around those kinds of things. I do listen, you know." He smiled and pulled me up by the arm. "By the way, you're up next."

I shot him a confused look, but I let him pull me towards the stage. "What am I singing?"

Joseph grinned. "You'll like it. It's perfect." He shrugged at my scowl. "It's a show tune," he offered.

I rolled my eyes. "You're just embracing the stereotype, now."

"Yep." He gave me one last gentle shove onto the stage.

I grabbed hold of the mic and frowned when the sharp beat of a tango floated out of the speakers with the chanted intro. I recognized the song from *Chicago: the Musical.*

Perfect? This?

I met Joseph's eyes across the bar and I considered what he'd said. I thought about what the god with one hand said, and I remembered everything that had happened at the Center. I thought about Zaro and turned it all over in my mind, looking at it from a different angle.

And it fit.

I nodded at Joseph and turned my attention to the screen in front of me. I opened my mouth and belted out the first line.

"He had it comin'!"

View other Black Rose Writing titles at www.blackrosewriting.com/books

and use promo code PRINT to receive a 20% discount when purchasing.

BLACK ROSE
writing™

www.ingramcontent.com/pod-product-compliance
Lightning Source LLC
Chambersburg PA
CBHW010448100726
47904CB00008B/2526

* 9 7 8 1 6 1 2 9 6 9 7 3 2 *